BLONDIE

and Dagwood's Snapshot Clue

BLONDIE

and

Dagwood's Snapshot Clue

An original story about
THE BUMSTEAD FAMILY
of the famous newspaper comics, radio series,
and motion pictures
"BLONDIE"

By CHIC YOUNG

WILDSIDE PRESS

TABLE OF CONTENTS

LIST OF ILLUSTRATIONS

LIST OF ILLUSTRATIONS

Dagwood Took Pictures From Every Angle

BLONDIE

and

Dagwood's Snapshot Clue

CHAPTER ONE

CRASH!

The moment Blondie made the remark, she regretted it. She could see that it had fired the imagination of her husband, Dagwood Bumstead, and when that happened, it usually meant trouble ahead for their otherwise peaceful household.

"That's right, Blondie, you're absolutely right," Dagwood said, his eyes shining. He was holding a small black camera in a manner which indicated he regarded it as a treasured possession.

"This little old black box is almost human. It's always doing us favors, but I'll bet it could get us into trouble, too, without half trying."

"Just like you, Dagwood," Blondie sighed. "You don't even need to *half* try, and zoom—we're knee-deep. . . ."

"Aw, Blondie," Dagwood muttered, taking himself and the camera out the back door, while Blondie's troubled gaze followed him. She heard him call his son, Alexander, and she smiled. Through the kitchen window, patient little Alexander could be seen reluctantly climbing onto a box.

13

"Can I go now?" the boy inquired after a long interval.

"Stand still and smile . . . Oh, boy, I'm getting some swell angles," Dagwood said. He was bending backwards at a forty-five degree angle. Suddenly, he yelled, "Blondie, Blondie, *quick!* I can't stand up straight!"

"Oh, my goodness!" Blondie exclaimed, and ran next door to get Mr. Woodley, their neighbor. Blondie grasped Dagwood under the arms.

"Pull hard," she instructed Mr. Woodley, who grabbed Dagwood around the calves of his legs. "He throws himself out of joint, taking all those tricky angle shots."

They heard a distinct snap, and Mr. Woodley said, "He's okay now."

Blondie picked up the camera and started toward the door.

"Aw, please give me my camera, dear," Dagwood pleaded.

"Nothing doing. That's the third time today you've done that."

Then she had a better idea. "I'll let you have your camera if you'll take Cookie for a ride around the block in her carriage."

"I might just as well leave the camera at home," Dagwood grumbled.

"You could take Cookie's picture over on Third

Street, Dagwood," Blondie suggested brightly. "I don't believe we have one single picture of Cookie on Third Street."

Dagwood grinned at her, his affectionate glance indicating that he knew she was bossing him around, but he didn't mind in the least.

So Dagwood had his camera with him when he started out for a walk with his baby daughter, Cookie, who looked more like her pretty mother every day. Dagwood walked proudly down the street. He didn't mind if some of the fellows jokingly called him "Mother" Bumstead.

He heard soft footsteps padding along behind him. Turning, he discovered the Bumstead dog, Daisy, and her family of five puppies. They were following sedately at a short distance.

"Daisy, you take your gang up some other street!" Dagwood ordered, anxiously looking about to see if any of the fellows had seen him leading the puppy parade. Daisy cast a reproachful look in Dagwood's direction, then haughtily turned and led her obedient followers in the opposite direction.

Nearing the corner of Third Street and Grand Avenue, Dagwood glanced at his tiny daughter. She smiled sweetly at him.

"What a picture!" Dagwood exclaimed. "Hold that pose, Cookie!"

Dagwood whipped out his camera, and squinted

through the view-finder. He stepped back a few inches, then clicked the shutter.

"Aw, shucks, Cookie, it won't be any good. Two cars *would* have to loom up right behind you just as I snapped that!"

Bending over the camera to move the film, Dagwood almost dropped it when he heard a deafening crash. He leaped protectively to Cookie's side before glancing up to see what had happened.

His mouth dropped open in amazement. One automobile had climbed over the curb at the corner, and crashed into a lamppost. Another was smack up against it, front fenders touching. Someone had rushed up to look into the car crumpled up against the post.

Dagwood's face lit up with inspiration, but he looked dubiously at Cookie.

"This is nothing for little girls to see," he said. "But papa is going to take some pictures."

He turned the baby carriage around to hide the view of the accident from the wide-eyed child. Then he aimed his camera at the collision scene. As he snapped the picture, the second car pulled away and sped down the street. Dagwood was not sure that he had caught it in the picture. He quickly advanced the film, and took three more pictures of the wrecked car against the lamppost. A crowd was gathering and a policeman had taken charge.

Among the children running up to see what the commotion was all about were Alexander and his playmate, Alvin. A woman, grasping her small daughter's hand, was hurrying away. As she passed Dagwood, she said, "That's no sight for children. They think the woman at the wheel is dying."

Dagwood forgot about taking any more pictures.

"Alexander! Alvin!" he called. The boys waved at him.

He gestured for them to come over to him.

"Hi, Pop!" Alexander said. "Did you get some pictures?"

"Yep," Dagwood said. "But I think we'd all better go back now."

"But, gee, we haven't seen anything yet," Alexander wailed.

"That's good," Dagwood said. "Come along now. Let's go home and have a sandwich."

Alvin and Alexander exchanged glances.

At that moment, a woman broke away from the throng gathered about the car. She was crying hysterically, and waving her arms. She rushed blindly in the direction of Dagwood and the carriage. Dagwood moved quickly to stand in front of the vehicle. The woman dashed toward him, and violently bumped into him. Dagwood tried to guard against the unexpected onslaught, and the camera flew out of his hands.

Kicking his foot out behind him, he sent the baby buggy moving along the sidewalk out of harm's way. The carriage was out of danger, but Dagwood definitely was not. He fell over backwards and the woman fell, too, her elbows punching his stomach and almost knocking him unconscious.

It took him a minute to catch his breath, but then he righted himself and helped the woman to her feet. Her face was distorted with emotion. He peered closely at her, but she turned her head after one wild-eyed glance, jerked her arm free from his hand, and ran across the street, where she quickly disappeared in the crowd.

"Whew!" Dagwood said, wiping his brow. He moved quickly to see if Cookie was all right, then he looked for the boys.

"Are you okay, Pop?" Alexander anxiously questioned him.

"I—I guess so," Dagwood replied, brushing himself off. Then he added, ruefully, "My camera is probably wrecked."

"Oh, no!" Alexander said. "Look, I caught it when it flew out of your hand."

Hastily examining it and finding it intact, Dagwood approvingly thumped Alexander on the back.

"Quick-thinking and quick-acting, just like your father," Dagwood beamed. Then he added, "Let's get out of here before another tornado hits me."

"You promised us sandwiches," Alvin reminded
him.

The two boys walked along with Dagwood as he
pushed Cookie toward home.

"That sure was funny the way that lady barged
into you, Mr. Bumstead," Alvin commented.

"Funny! She knocked him down. What's funny
about that?" Alexander demanded.

"Alvin means it was peculiar," Dagwood put in.
"Isn't that what you meant, Alvin?"

"Yeah. It was funny . . ." he began.

"It wasn't funny," Alexander interrupted.

"It was what your Pop said," Alvin conceded.

Dagwood stopped suddenly. "Tell me why you
think so, Alvin," he said.

"Well, she was standing there with all the others."

"I saw her standing there, too. She was looking
at us," Alexander said.

"You mean looking at your Pop," Alvin corrected.
"Then she starts yelling."

"And running," Alexander said.

"And headed right for me," Dagwood said, frowning.

"Maybe she's crazy," Alexander added, cheerfully.

Alvin seemed delighted with that idea. "Maybe
she'll follow you home."

Dagwood jerked his head around and looked be
hind him. There were several persons leaving the

scene of the crash and walking along behind him. Instead of turning at the next corner, Dagwood continued straight ahead, crossing the street.

"Aw, gee, I thought we were going home for sandwiches," Alexander complained.

"We're going to take a walk first," Dagwood said. The boys held a brief consultation.

"We'll see you later," Alexander called, as he and Alvin began running toward home. Dagwood nodded and waved.

He tucked the buggy blanket around Cookie. "After we get to the corner, we'll double back, Cookie. We'll soon find out if that woman is following us."

Dagwood walked two blocks out of his way, then doubled back. Cookie was beginning to get restless. Uneasy though he was, Dagwood knew he would have to head for home. He peered cautiously up and down before turning into the Bumstead yard. There were one or two men in sight, but no women. Dagwood began to feel a trifle silly. What would he tell Blondie? He decided it would be better not to try to explain his sudden decision to take a long walk.

"Boy, did I get some pictures!" he exclaimed, before Blondie could say a word.

"Of Cookie?" she asked, eagerly.

"Well, er, not exactly," Dagwood said, lamely.

Dagwood Walked Two Blocks out of His Way

"Of Alexander?"

"No. A car hit a lamppost and I took pictures of
it," he blurted out.

"Whatever for?" Blondie demanded. "We don't
want to clutter up our nice picture album with people's wrecked cars, do we?"

Blondie was busily removing Cookie's coat as she
spoke.

"I guess you don't understand," Dagwood sighed.
"If artists only painted pictures of themselves and
their families, we'd think they were selfish, wouldn't
we?"

Blondie's candid eyes appraised him. "Whatever
does that have to do with . . ."

"Besides, maybe I can sell them," Dagwood said.

"Sell them?" Blondie was frankly puzzled. "Do
you mean people go around buying snapshots of accidents as though they were works of art?"

"Of course not," Dagwood scoffed. "But I know
a fellow who lives on a federal highway where there
are a lot of accidents and he makes lots of money
taking pictures of them and selling them to insurance companies. He's sort of a silent witness."

"Hmmnn," Blondie pondered.

Happy to have caught her interest, Dagwood
plunged along with his recital. He began to wave
his arms dramatically.

"These will be especially valuable in my eyes,

dear, because I possess them at considerable risk to my person."

"You what?" exclaimed the astonished Blondie. Alexander, who had been quietly standing in the doorway, spoke up.

"Daddy was blitzed," he said.

Blondie looked from one to the other in complete bewilderment. Dagwood, with his big, bland face, with the two big tufts of hair sticking straight out from his pompadour, beamed at her. Alexander, a small copy of the same model, had an identical expression on his young face.

"Let's all sit down on the davenport and talk the whole thing over quietly and calmly," Blondie said soothingly.

"There's nothing to it, Mom," Alexander said, glancing anxiously toward the front door, and edging closer to it. "Pop was at the corner when the car got banged against the post, took some pictures of it, and a woman who'd been watching him started to yell and ran for him."

Blondie turned to Dagwood. "Ran for you, dear?" she asked with ominous calm.

Hastily, Dagwood explained how he was completely taken by surprise when a perfectly strange woman, in wild hysteria, flew at him and knocked him down.

"What did she look like?" Blondie demanded,

looking from her son to her husband in a bewildered manner.

"Gosh," Dagwood said, scratching his head. "She had on a green coat. Her face was all screwed up like this." He made a face intended to show deep emotion, which sent Alexander into gales of laughter.

"She had mouse-colored hair. And high heels. I remember that, because one of them dug into my foot."

"Tell her about me catching the camera," Alexander suggested.

Dagwood patted Alexander. "Alexander caught the camera."

"What do you mean—were you throwing it around?" Blondie asked.

Dagwood and Alexander laughed. "No—it flew out of my hands when that woman in the green coat barged into me."

Blondie didn't join in the laughter. A serious expression creased a slight frown between her lovely eyes, which were suddenly, unaccountably, filled with fear.

She said, slowly, "Dagwood, I—I wish you had not been around at that moment. I wish you had not taken pictures . . ."

"Poof! It's my lucky day, I'll betcha," he scoffed, and laughed. But the laugh had a false note in it.

And Alexander didn't laugh. He knew, and Dagwood knew, that Blondie's premonitions were nothing to be lightly brushed aside. Involuntarily, Blondie shuddered.

CHAPTER TWO

AN UNWELCOME CALLER

Dagwood seated himself at the writing desk.

"Are you going to catch up on your letter writing, dear?" Blondie inquired.

"Not now. I think I'll write out a report of the accident while it's still fresh in my mind."

Then he shouted, "*Blondie!* Have you been using my fountain pen? It won't write."

"Yes, dear," she answered. "I used it to write some letters."

"Well, when it ran dry, why didn't you fill it?"

"I did fill it," she said, impatience creeping into her voice.

"It won't write!" Dagwood complained! "What kind of ink did you use?"

"We didn't have any ink, so I made some out of blueberry jam and water," his smiling wife informed him.

Dagwood gritted his teeth, restrained himself from going into a rage, buried his head in his arms and murmured, "Give me strength."

He knew Blondie meant to be helpful, but her wifely little gesture had probably ruined the fountain pen. Dagwood threw it back on the desk and

26

abandoned the idea of making out an accident report. He did so with apparent reluctance, mumbling something to the effect that he would probably be sorry later.

"After that long walk, it's going to be good to get my slippers on and sit down and read my new magazine," he commented. "Blondie, will you please bring my slippers?"

That request, too, brought only disappointment.

"Oh, darling, I forgot to tell you!" Blondie said. "The puppies chewed up your slippers today, and I threw them away."

"Well, where's my magazine?" Dagwood asked, irritably.

"Oh, my goodness—I loaned it to Mrs. Fuddle and she didn't return it," Blondie explained.

There was a hint of sarcasm in Dagwood's voice when he said, "Well, anyway, it's good to sit down."

But he was too restless to sit still for long. The afternoon's excitement had been too much for him. He paced the floor a few times, then turned a speculative eye toward the davenport. A minute later, he snuggled down on its soft cushions. Just as his eyes closed, a voice spoke behind him.

"Is Alexander at home, Mr. Bumstead?" It was Alvin.

Dagwood groaned. "The minute I lie down for a little well-deserved nap, somebody comes in and wakes me up. I work and slave all day, until I'm worn and haggard and what happens? I'm even denied the simple pleasure of a moment's relaxation. Is there no rest? Must I go through life with a body all aching and wracked with pain. . . ."

He turned around. Alvin was not in sight. "Alvin, where are you?"

Dagwood got up and went to the door just in time to see Alvin walking out.

"You're no gentleman!" Dagwood scolded. "You could've waited until I finished talking!"

"All I wanted was to know if Alexander was at home," Alvin said, hurrying away.

As Dagwood slammed the door, he heard light laughter behind him.

Blondie had been listening, and she giggled, "After all, Dagwood, he didn't ask for a lecture."

Sheepishly, Dagwood grinned. "Well, I hope it's a lesson to him," he said. His glance rested on the hall table where he had placed the camera, and an animated expression crossed his face.

"Gosh! I almost forgot about the pictures!" he exclaimed.

Blondie said, hastily, "Dagwood, I wish you *would* forget about them."

"Not on your sweet life," Dagwood said. "Who knows—maybe I can sell them for enough to buy a movie camera. I'd better put this little black box in a good, safe place until I get time to develop the films."

"And who is going to hand you all of this good money?" Blondie asked.

"Why—er—why, the people who were in the accident," he declared. "Or the insurance companies."

Blondie looked at him, a smile playing about her lips. "You no doubt know their names," she said, slyly.

"Gosh!" Dagwood muttered. "I never thought of that!" He grabbed his coat and hat, and *swish*—he bounded out the door and down the street.

"Where's Daddy going in such a big hurry?" asked Alexander, appearing from the back yard.

"I think he's going back to the scene of that crash," Blondie explained. "And if he's lucky, he'll be too late."

"What do you mean 'if he's lucky'?" Alexander asked.

"I can't explain it, son, but—I just know that the less he gets mixed up in it, the better off we will all be," Blondie said.

Alexander regarded her, frankly puzzled, then shrugged his shoulders and ran away to resume his play in the back yard.

Dagwood hurried toward the intersection where the car had smashed into the post. The wrecked vehicle was nowhere to be seen. He rushed over to the spot, where a man seemed to be explaining the accident to a few strangers.

"Which way did they go?" Dagwood asked, panting for breath.

"Who?" the man inquired.

"Why—the people—the car—the accident, you know. Who was it? Who did it?" Words tumbled out, as Dagwood grasped the man by the lapels.

The man roughly brushed Dagwood's hands aside. "What business is it of yours, young man?" His piercing black eyes were turned full on Dagwood, who gulped and paused to get control of himself. Then Dagwood became wary.

"Well—er, I just wondered if it was anybody I knew," he said.

"Oh, you did, did you? Are you *sure?* You wouldn't by any chance be a hit-and-run driver, would you? You certainly look capable of being one."

"Oh, no!" Dagwood said, aghast. "I saw—" Abruptly, he changed his mind about what he was going to say. Instead, he started to stroll away. "I heard someone say it was a bus and a truck. I know the bus driver."

"Well, it wasn't!" the gimlet-eyed stranger barked. Then he added, "As if YOU didn't know."

Dagwood assumed an attitude of wide-eyed innocence. "It wasn't?" he asked, and quickly walked away. The man's belligerent attitude upset him. Dagwood turned around to take a good look at him.

"I don't like dark, swarthy men," he said in an undertone. "Especially when they wear loud striped suits."

"Were you addressing me?" said a woman's voice.

"No, ma'am," Dagwood said, turning to her. Then he stared. It was the same woman, wearing a green coat, who had hysterically run toward him right after the accident. She was looking at him inquiringly, her attitude indicating that she had never seen him before in her life.

Dagwood backed away, and followed his first impulse—to run as fast as possible toward home. He ventured a backward glance, and observed that she remained standing there, her amazed expression suggesting that she thought *he* was crazy. In a fleeting survey, Dagwood also noticed that the man in the striped suit, and the group near him, had the same impression. One man, pointing at Dagwood, then tapping his temple with a forefinger, sorrowfully shook his head. But Dagwood was too intent on getting away to stop to correct that impression.

"Maybe I *am* crazy," he panted, as he dashed up his own front steps.

Blondie hurried from the kitchen to see what the commotion was about. She found Dagwood peeking through the curtains of the front window.

"Sh—sh," he said, his finger to his lips. His wife watched him as he peered through the curtains, first in one direction and then in the other. She kept silent for awhile, but finally had to know what was happening.

"Is someone following you?" she whispered, her eyes wide with excitement.

"That's what I'm trying to find out," Dagwood blurted.

Satisfied that there was ño one lurking in the vicinity, Dagwood left the window and sank into the nearest chair, completely exhausted.

"I'll make you a cup of coffee, dear, and then you can tell me all about it," Blondie soothed. "You may also have one of the sandwiches left over from my bridge party yesterday."

"You mean those fancy doo-dads . . ."

"Yes, dear. Shredded carrot salad with chopped cherries and marshmallow, lettuce and raisin sandwiches with mayonnaise and frozen prune whip," she explained.

"Do you want to *poison* me?"

Blondie pouted. "The women ate the sandwiches and said they were delicious."

"Well, women are stronger than men!" Dagwood declared.

Blondie glared at him. "You're all upset, Dagwood," she said. "I'll bring the coffee."

"You Can Tell Me All About It," Blondie Soothed

Dagwood was lost in the depths of despair when Blondie reappeared. She sensed that his dash to the scene of the accident had been unsuccessful.

"You tried, Dagwood," she said. "It isn't your fault if you couldn't get any information. Was there anyone there?"

For a moment he was silent, debating whether to tell her all the details. She looked at him expectantly, and at the same time sympathetically. She put her arm across Dagwood's shoulder as though he were young Alexander with an irksome problem to be solved.

"Tell me, now," Blondie said, coaxingly. "Who did you think was following you?"

"It might have been either of them," Dagwood said. "It could have been the man in the striped suit, or the woman who flew into me."

"Now start from the beginning, Dagwood," Blondie suggested. "Begin from the moment you approached the corner of Third Street and Grand Avenue."

Crinkling up his brow in deep thought, Dagwood tried to recall everything. He explained about the damaged car having been taken away, and described the swarthy man who had been talking and gesticulating to the group gathered at the spot where the accident had occurred.

"Of course, I thought he must know all about it,

because his mouth was going jabber, jabber, jabber."

"What did he tell you?"

Dagwood scowled. "Instead of answering *my*
question, he turned on me, and started questioning
me. He acted as though he thought *I* had something
to do with the blamed old accident. He said, right
out in front of everybody, that I looked like a hit-
and-run driver!"

Blondie was indignant. "How could he dare think
such a horrible thing. If I were you, I'd have been
tempted to punch him in the nose. What did you do,
Dagwood?"

Momentarily taken aback by her vehemence, Dagwood tried to remember.

"He—er—he wasn't the type that a guy would care
to pick a fight with," he said, earnestly. "And besides, I thought I'd better use my brains instead of
my brawn. I just trumped up an explanation, and
walked away. And guess who was standing so close
to me that I almost fell over her?"

"That same woman who ran into you?" Blondie
said calmly.

"That's right," Dagwood nodded.

"Did she apologize or explain?"

"No. That's the strange part of it. She looked at
me blankly. If she remembered having seen me before, she certainly didn't show it! She seemed to

think I was batty. And the man in the striped suit seemed to think I was batty. And the people around him seemed to think I was batty. Then *I* began to think I was batty, and ran home. After I got here, I wondered if any of them had followed me."

His reference to being followed sent Blondie hurrying to the window.

"There doesn't seem to be anyone out there now," she said.

"That's what I thought when I looked. But, of course, if anyone followed me, he or she could easily duck between the houses to keep out of my sight."

The Bumsteads exchanged uneasy glances.

Blondie was the first to regain her composure. "Let's just forget about it, shall we?"

"I can try," Dagwood said. "Guess I'll go upstairs and take a bath."

"Cookie's asleep. I'll run over to the grocery store."

"I'm going to think of a way to find out more about that accident," Dagwood vowed.

"Must you, Dagwood? Can't you forget it?"

"No. I still think it was a stroke of luck to get those pictures."

He was halfway up the stairs, and failed to hear Blondie's parting remark.

"It was a stroke of luck—*bad* luck, I'm afraid," she said.

Dagwood had finished bathing, and was starting to dress when he heard Alexander come into the house. A moment later, the doorbell rang.

Alexander bounded up the steps, and informed his father, "There's a gentleman at the door who wants to see you."

"Did you invite him in?" Dagwood wanted to know.

"No, I didn't, Daddy," Alexander replied.

"That's not polite. You should always ask our friends to come in and wait." Alexander began to descend the steps. "Now ask him to come in and be seated. Give him one of my cigars and tell him I'll be right down," Dagwood continued.

Alexander said, "Okay."

While he finished dressing, Dagwood began to think. Who was downstairs? Could it be someone connected with the accident case? If it was not, who would be calling at this unusual hour?

Dagwood straightened his tie, brushed his suit-coat, and sedately walked downstairs to greet his caller. He paused at the door, mouth agape, as he spotted his visitor. Relaxed among the davenport cushions, comfortably smoking one of Dagwood's best cigars, was the most obnoxious-looking hobo Dagwood had ever seen. Ragged and dirty, the old tramp beamed at Dagwood, grinning a toothless grin through a long, black bristly beard. The master of the Bumstead homestead lost no time in ushering his unwelcome guest to the door.

Before Dagwood could begin his scolding, Alexander said, "I did as you told me, Daddy. I invited him to make himself at home and offered him a cigar. You can't say I'm not polite."

Blondie chose that moment to walk into the house.

"Dagwood, what do you mean by such actions? The very idea, letting that dirty old bum into our nice clean house."

"Pfft! pfft!" Dagwood was so angry that he couldn't speak intelligibly. Alexander quickly explained what had happened, ending by boasting, "But Daddy threw him out."

"Goodness me," Blondie complained. "I can't leave for one second without something queer going on around here. I'm just surprised that your father didn't keep him here long enough to take a picture of him."

Alexander laughed. "That's funny, Mama. That gentleman mentioned pictures. He wanted to know if I knew where Daddy kept his camera."

Dagwood held his breath, then sighed with relief when his son said, "But I told him he could ask Daddy when he came down."

"He wanted to see Daddy's camera, did he?" Excitement tinged Blondie's tone. "I think I know what that means."

"What?" Dagwood demanded.

"It means that isn't the last we'll see of your crummy-looking visitor."

CHAPTER THREE

"I've got it! I've got it!" Dagwood exclaimed, jumping up from the chair, where he had apparently been in deep thought.

Blondie waited for an explanation.

"I can tack up a sign on the lamppost where the accident took place, inviting interested parties to get in touch with me if they want information about the crash."

"Suppose the 'interested parties' included that woman and the man in the striped suit?"

"Gosh! That's right! How could I find out who is mixed up in it, without having them find out who I am and mixing *me* up in it?" he wondered. "Do you suppose I could put the sign up without my name on it, and see who reads it?"

"No, silly. Everyone who goes near there will stop to read it."

"Well, doggone!" Dagwood complained. "There must be *some* way to figure this business out."

"Think, Dagwood. Where would you look if you were trying to get information?"

Alexander had been standing in the doorway, listening to the discussion.

"Daddy would look in the paper."

Dagwood said, "In the—that's right, Alexander. I was about to say that I would look in the paper. In the personal column."

"Eureka! That's what I'll do! I'll put in a blind ad, and one of the insurance companies will be sure to get in touch with me. Maybe two of them will. Then I can sell my pictures to the highest bidder."

Blondie patted Alexander approvingly, and he smiled at her when Dagwood said, "The paper! I'm glad I thought of it."

He scurried around, trying to find paper and pencil, getting more and more enthusiastic about the plan.

"They won't know who I am," he said, "and that will keep out undesirable characters. Is it too late to get an ad in the newspaper today?"

"The newsboy will deliver the paper in a few minutes, Dagwood," Blondie patiently pointed out. "You might find some news in it about the accident. Had you thought of that?"

"Why—why, of course, I thought of that right away." He walked to the window and looked anxiously up and down the street, grumbling about the slowness of the newsboy. Then he called in a hoarse whisper, "Blondie! Look down the street!"

Blondie hurried to his side. "It's that tramp, Dagwood! What do you suppose he is standing over there for?"

Alexander spoke up. "Shall I ask him?"

"Heavens, no. You stay right here!" his mother ordered. "Dagwood, maybe you ought to stroll over there and ask him why he is staying around this neighborhood."

"Who, me? He's an American citizen, Blondie, and has a perfect right to stand there if he wants to stand there. He's standing there on his constitutional rights. A person can't go up to another person, and demand to know. . . ."

"Never mind making a speech, Dagwood," Blondie interrupted. "I would like to know what he's doing there. It seems to me he is glancing over here out of the corner of his eye."

"He probably wants to come back here to rest on our davenport and smoke another cigar," Dagwood grinned. "He'd probably appreciate an invitation to dine, too."

"He isn't going to get one!" Blondie said.

"He's going away now," Dagwood said, after another survey of the street. "All that fuss over nothing."

"I hope you're right," said Blondie dubiously.

"What was I doing? Oh, I remember. I was about to compose an advertisement for the paper."

Dagwood sat at the desk and wrote busily for a few minutes. Blondie suggested that it might be

Dagwood Sat Down at the Desk and Wrote Busily

wise to wait until the paper got there, but Dagwood was concentrating on his writing and paid no attention. Finally he turned around, very pleased with his efforts.

"How's this, Blondie?" he asked proudly. " 'Will person or persons interested in obtaining snapshots of accident at Third Street and Grand Avenue get in touch with writer of this ad.' "

"That sounds all right, Dagwood, but—" Blondie began.

"I'll run down to the corner and mail it right this minute," her husband said enthusiastically. He grabbed his coat and hat from the clothes closet, and swish—Dagwood was out the door before Blondie could speak another word.

"But Dagwood," she called. "Suppose the pictures aren't any good?"

With an airy wave of his hand he brushed off that possibility.

"Why don't you wait until the paper gets here?" Blondie shouted. "I think the boy is at the end of the block."

But by that time the sprinting Dagwood was out of hearing distance.

Blondie went back into the house. She heard someone at the door a few minutes later. It was Mr. Beasley, the postman.

"Did you see Dagwood, Mr. Beasley?" Blondie

asked. "He had a letter he wanted to mail right away."

"He probably got to the corner box in time to catch the mail truck. But I found your puppies up the street, Blondie." He deposited his armload of wriggling puppies in the front hall.

"Oh, thanks, Mr. Beasley. Wait a moment."

She held Cookie out to him. "Take care of Cookie for me a moment, will you please?" she asked. "I must run over to see Mrs. Woodley."

He nodded, and she left him with Cookie. In a few minutes she returned and she thanked him. The postman tipped his hat politely. "It's all part of the service," he said.

Dagwood was on his way home from the mailbox when Alexander and Alvin stopped him. There was tragedy in their young faces.

"Pop," Alexander wailed, "my kite's caught up on Mrs. Schroeder's second floor porch."

"Why, I'll get it for you in a jiffy," his father replied. He looked up to see that the kite was tangled in the telephone wires near the porch. While the boys gazed at him in admiration, Dagwood climbed up the porch, and then, grasping the porch rail with one hand, stretched out to reach the kite. He was leaning in front of Mr. Schroeder's open window, and Mr. Schroeder chose that moment to look out.

Poised in midair, Dagwood faced him, and said, "Hello, Mr. Schroeder, how are you?"

The neighbor answered, "Fine, thank you." Then he popped his head back into the room.

Dagwood reached again for the kite, and almost lost his grip on the railing when Mr. Schroeder's head popped out the window again. "Say, did you climb up here just to ask me that?" Mr. Schroeder demanded.

Dagwood shook his head negatively, and pointed at the kite, while Alvin and Alexander were convulsed with mirth. With as much dignity as he could muster, Dagwood climbed back down with the kite, and told the boys to run off and play.

Blondie's remark about the possibility of the accident films not being any good kept troubling Dagwood. He told himself he'd have to hurry down to his basement darkroom and develop them, to prove she was wrong. He had quite a few films piled up, mostly pictures of the children and the puppies, which he could start on to make sure that the developing chemicals, the light, and the printing paper were right. He was turning over the process in his mind when he entered the house.

At first glance, he thought he was alone, and the davenport cushions seemed to be whispering a soft invitation. Before he could accept, he heard Blondie's voice from the rear of the house.

"The evening paper is here, Dagwood," she said. When she came into the living room, she was shaking her head in reproach. "You should have listened to me, and waited a few minutes. Then there would have been no necessity to insert that ad."

"Is there something in the paper about the accident?" Dagwood asked eagerly.

"There's quite an item about it. On the front page, too."

"Where? Where?" Dagwood scanned the top headlines.

"Down in the corner," Blondie pointed out. "The headline reads 'CAR RAMS LAMPPOST. WOMAN DRIVER KILLED.' "

Dagwood hastily read the newspaper account, beginning:

"A freak accident at the corner of Third Street and Grand Avenue today cost the life of Mrs. Rufus Tyvand Billingate, wealthy socialite, of Brentwood Manor, Shorecrest Park. According to three eyewitnesses, the crash victim apparently lost control of the wheel as she attempted to make a right turn from Third Street to Grand Avenue. Investigation proved the deceased wore eyeglasses of unusual thickness, and police are of the opinion that they were responsible for the miscalculation of distance."

Puzzled, Dagwood looked from the newspaper to Blondie. "That's odd, Blondie. They don't say a word about the other car."

"Read the rest of it," Blondie suggested.

The article continued:

"With the exception of one nephew, Mrs. Billingate was the only survivor of a pioneer family."

Dagwood commented, "It doesn't give his name."

"Oh, yes, after the history of the family, it tells about the funeral arrangements being taken care of by her nephew, Horace Tyvand and his wife, who recently moved here from Gainsborough to make their home at Brentwood Manor with the late Mrs. Billingate."

"Well, that simplifies it. All I need do is call him up," Dagwood said.

"But you can't now," Blondie said. "Listen to this: 'Mr. and Mrs. Tyvand, according to servants at the Manor, were out of town at the time of the crash. They wired instructions, and will arrive in the city by tomorrow night.' "

Dagwood shook his head in bewilderment. "Let me read that first part over again," he said. " 'According to the three eyewitnesses, the crash victim apparently lost control of the wheel. Then it says something about 'miscalculation of distance.' That's funny. That isn't the way it looked to *me*. I was an eyewitness, too."

"You might have imagined that you saw the other car, Dagwood," Blondie said. "Otherwise, at least one of the three others would have noticed it, too."

"But I know positively that I didn't imagine it, Blondie!" Dagwood was becoming exasperated. "I guess I know when I see something with my own eyes whether I'm looking at it or not!"

"Don't shout, dear," Blondie soothed. "I'm not trying to start an argument with you. All I know is what I read in the paper."

"And you would believe that before you would believe me." By this time, Dagwood was waving his arms. "Your own husband tells you what *he* saw, and just because three other people saw something else, you think you should take their word against mine."

"Please, Dagwood, calm down," Blondie said. "I only meant to point out—"

"What's more, I'm going to call up the police right this minute. We'll see who is to be believed and who isn't—"

"Wait, Dagwood. You're too excited now."

"Excited? Excited? Who's excited?" Dagwood shouted, pacing up and down and gesticulating wildly. "Where's the phone, where's the phone?"

He pranced over to the telephone, and demanded gruffly, "Police station."

Blondie hovered over him nervously as he talked.

"Hello!" Dagwood shouted into the telephone. "Is this the police station? This is Dagwood Bumstead. And I want to tell you that it's all a big lie . . . What those three witnesses said . . . the three who told about the accident . . . No, no . . . I'm not in an accident . . . No . . . No . . . I don't want to report an accident . . . It was reported . . . It was in the paper . . . No, I'm not a reporter . . . Listen, willya? . . . Who's a crank? . . . Lissen, here, you're a servant of the public and you can't call good tax-paying citizens screwballs! . . . Let me tell you . . ." There was a "click," and Dagwood put the receiver on the hook. Blondie was standing there, arms folded, impatiently tapping her foot.

"He hung up," Dagwood said, furiously.

"Small wonder!" Blondie said. "You're lucky they didn't send the paddy wagon for you, dear."

"What should I do now?" He asked the question in the tone of a small boy earnestly seeking advice. Blondie regarded him appraisingly, then she smiled.

"You take a nice nap, now, Dagwood, while I think about it. We mustn't be too hasty." She cast a meaningful glance in the direction of the telephone. Dagwood obediently lay on the davenport, confident that Blondie would think of a solution. He had time only to close his eyes, when Alexander came in.

"A man at the door wants to see you, Daddy," he

announced.

"What does he want?" Dagwood growled.

"He wants to sell you something."

"Tell him I'm away on a hunting expedition in Africa."

As Alexander turned to deliver the message, Dagwood sat up. "No, don't say that! That wouldn't be the truth and I wouldn't want you to tell a falsehood."

Dagwood resumed his napping position, and added, "Just say I'm not at home." A startled expression crossed his son's face, but with a shrug the boy went to pass on the information to the salesman. It dawned on Dagwood that Alexander would still be telling a fib, but it was too late then to call him back. He lay back against the pillows.

Dagwood twisted and turned. He could not rest. He was beginning to get hungry.

"How long will it be before supper, Blondie?" he called.

"About two minutes. You'll just have time to wash your hands," his wife answered. Dagwood ran upstairs, scrubbed his hands, and came down again saying, "Ah-h, I still have a minute left for a quick nap."

Before his head hit the cushion, Blondie said, "Supper's ready."

"Gee, that minute went fast," Dagwood complained.

During the meal, Dagwood asked, timidly, "Did you think of what to do yet, Blondie?"

"I haven't thought it all out yet, Dagwood. But I think the whole business can wait until we've slept on it."

"What about the pictures?"

"That's right. I almost forgot about them. Are you too tired to work on them tonight?"

"No-oo, I'm not too tired. But I want to be sure to do a good job of it. I'll develop and print some old films first, to be sure. I want to be positive in advance that I won't be disturbed."

Blondie promised to let him work undisturbed on condition that he help her do the dishes and put the children and the puppies to bed. While Dagwood was washing dishes, Alexander asked, "Papa, will you help me with my homework?"

"Yes, dear, as soon as I finish the dishes," his father answered. Before he could finish, Blondie came in with the baby.

"Dagwood," she asked, "will you hold Cookie while I look up those bills you have to pay tomorrow?"

"Sure," Dagwood said. He stood there, wearing an apron, holding Cookie, and facing a sinkful of dishes. "And a fellow asked me the other day if I was married!" he muttered.

"Will You Help Me With My Homework?"
Alexander Asked

Blondie laughed. "It isn't as bad as all that, dear!" She took command of the dishwashing, and in a few minutes everything was spic and span. Then the children were hiked off to bed, and Daisy led her five puppies to their sleeping quarters.

Everything was peaceful and quiet in the Bumstead household.

"You should be able to work in your darkroom, now, Dagwood. I'll go over to Woodleys' for a little while. If you need me for anything, you can call me there."

"Stay as late as you like," Dagwood said. "But I wish you wouldn't tell them about the accident. Promise?"

"I promise," Blondie said, solemnly. "But I don't see any reason for being so secretive about it," she added.

"I don't want the Woodleys saying I'm a screwball, too!" Dagwood informed her, and he gave her an affectionate hug as she left.

He went into the hall, where he had last seen his camera. It wasn't on the stand, nor was it in the desk. Then he recalled that he had planned to put it in a good place, mentioned it in front of Blondie, and assumed that Blondie had put it away for him. He was about to call her, but decided instead to go down to the basement, get everything ready, and prepare to develop the films, trying out a few old ones first. If she were not home by that time, he could call the Woodleys' and ask where Blondie had put the camera.

Dagwood enjoyed the process of making pictures, and had a complete set of equipment. In addition to the chemicals, lights, pans, dryers, blotting books, and reflecting screen, he had a home-made enlarging box of which he was extremely proud. He was able to "blow up" a film to any size and see an enlarged, detailed view of each picture before he made the prints.

He had a handful of films taken at a picnic. Some were amusing shots of Alexander and Cookie, and there were others of Daisy and the pups which made him laugh out loud. There was a particularly funny one of Elmer stuck in the mud, with the four sister puppies, concerned and helpless, gazing at him. Dagwood heard the creak of the basement step. Someone was coming downstairs.

"Don't turn on the light, Blondie. Come here and look at this negative of Elmer."

There was no answer, but Dagwood was certain he had heard footsteps.

"That's you, isn't it, Blondie?" he asked. There was a shade of apprehension in his voice. He reached behind him to touch Blondie's face. Instead of the smooth satin of her skin, he felt the rough, bearded face of a man. He clutched at the whiskers, and before he could cry out, a heavy blow from a club descended on his head, knocking him unconscious. He fell in a crumpled, helpless heap on the basement floor.

CHAPTER FOUR

A THOROUGH SEARCH

A voice which seemed to come from a long distance was saying over and over, "Dagwood, are you all right? Speak to me, dear!"

Dagwood trembled. There was something icy cold on his forehead and temples. Trickles of cold water ran into his ears and down the back of his neck. But the sound of Blondie's voice, coming closer and closer, warmed him. He opened his eyes and saw her sweet face, pale and strained, directly above him. She was sitting on the basement floor, holding his head in her lap, applying wet cloths to his aching head.

"W—what hit me?" he muttered in a small, weak voice.

"I don't know, Dagwood, unless something fell off a shelf while you were working."

He jerked to a sitting position, moaned "Owooooo!" and fell back again.

"Try to get up again, slowly, this time," Blondie advised.

Dagwood gradually raised himself, holding his head. He gazed around the room, still dazed.

"Nothing fell on me. I know that. Let me think."

Blondie told him that she had spent about an hour at the Woodleys' and then dropped back to see how he was getting along with the films.

"The lights were all turned on, but you didn't answer when I called down the basement stairway. I thought you might have gone to bed, forgetting to turn out the lights, as you sometimes do, Dagwood. When you weren't up there, I came back down here, and found you on the floor."

Dagwood shook his head experimentally. "I guess it's going to stay on," he commented, with a mirthless smile. "I remember now. It was dark in here, and I thought I heard you coming down the steps. Then I thought you were right behind me, but it was a man, and he clubbed me on the head with something hard."

"How did you know it was a man?" Blondie asked.

"His face was rough, and he had a beard." Dagwood looked at his hand, and then felt around on the floor.

"I found some!" he exclaimed.

"Some what?"

"Some of his whiskers, see? I knew I grabbed at them when I was falling." He held up a few strands of black, bristly whiskers. "What's more, I think I know where I've seen some just like them. Take a good look at them, Blondie. Do you remember seeing some like those before?"

After a careful scrutiny, Blondie cried, "That tramp! The one that Alexander invited to come in to make himself comfortable. He had whiskers like that!"

"Well, what do you know!" Dagwood said. "Do you suppose he resented being thrown out, and came back to 'get' me?"

Blondie shook her head. "No, Dagwood, I think it goes deeper than that. Let's look around, and see what's missing. Remember, he asked Alexander some questions about your camera, didn't he?"

"That's right." He glanced around the room, and noticed that there were film negatives scattered about on his worktable. Some of them, which had been clipped to a string and hung up to dry, apparently had been ripped down and then tossed to one side.

"Gosh, all those swell picnic pictures," Dagwood complained. Blondie looked into the enlarger and admired the film of Elmer and the other puppies. When Dagwood offered to turn off the other lights to give her a better view, she squealed "No," and then the thought dawned on both of them that whoever Dagwood's assailant was, he might still be in the house somewhere. Blondie clung to her husband, who was having trouble keeping his own knees from trembling.

"W-Whatever he was looking for, he didn't find it down here," Dagwood said, his voice quavering. "I—I guess we'd better go upstairs and see if anything is missing."

Blondie surprised him by bursting into unrestrained laughter. Then he laughed too, when she said they should check up to see if anyone had walked off with their six watch dogs.

"By the way, Blondie," Dagwood was suddenly serious. "What became of my camera? I saw it in the hall this afternoon, just before I went back to the scene of the accident."

"It should be in the clothes closet, on the hat shelf," Blondie said. They raced upstairs, into the hall, and opened the closet door. The camera was there, just where Blondie had put it. With a good deal of trepidation, Dagwood opened the back of it to see if the film pack was intact.

The Bumsteads sighed with relief to find that it had not been touched.

"The man who hit you over the head was probably looking for these, Dagwood," Blondie said. "That proves someone knows you took pictures of the accident."

"What did I tell you?" Dagwood was triumphant. "He probably wants to sell them to the insurance companies, too. They must be worth even more than I thought, or he wouldn't go to all that trouble of

They Found the Camera on the Closet Shelf

trying to get them."

Blondie didn't answer, as she thoughtfully paced back and forth.

"There's something rather queer about all this, Dagwood," she said. "Are you *positive* your memory isn't playing tricks on you? Why didn't the other witnesses get the same view of the accident that you did?"

"How should I know? They could have been coming from the other direction. Or maybe they weren't paying close attention," Dagwood declared.

"You weren't paying very close attention either, dear, taking a picture of Cookie."

Indignant and sputtering, Dagwood explained again how things appeared to him at the time of the crash, but his wife was busy with her own thoughts. Dagwood quieted down after a short interval, then strode over to the telephone. That attracted Blondie's attention.

"Who are you calling at this hour, Dagwood?" she asked.

"I'm going to call the police station again," Dagwood insisted. "I'm going to tell them that maybe those other witnesses that they interviewed didn't get a clear view."

Before Blondie could stop him, he had asked the operator for the police station.

"Please, Dagwood, wait until we talk it over," she

begged.

Dagwood waved her aside, saying into the mouth-piece, "Hello, police sergeant? This is Dagwood Bumstead . . . Bumstead. Yeah . . . You remember me? Well . . . er . . . yes, I'm that one . . . I just want-ed to tell you that maybe the three witnesses saw it from the other side. . . the accident . . . no, I wasn't in it . . . No, I saw it, and I didn't see what they saw . . . No! . . . What do you mean, am I touched in the head? How did you find out about me being hit on the head? You guessed it? . . . but, officer . . . just a minute, officer . . . yes, I remember . . . yes, sir . . . but sergeant, let me explain . . . no, sir . . . no, sir . . . goodnight, sir!"

"What did he say?" Blondie wanted to know, as she pushed the crestfallen Dagwood into an easy chair.

"I would get *that* guy on the line," Dagwood wailed. "He's the desk sergeant who was sorry be-cause he couldn't run me in last winter."

At first Blondie didn't know what he was talking about, but then it all came back to her. Blondie had called Dagwood from the bowling alley, when Alex-ander's foot got caught under the porch railing. He came in such a hurry that he forgot to leave the big, black, shiny bowling ball at the alley. Thinking he could pick it up on the way back, he rolled it into a drugstore as someone opened the door.

"Help! It's a *bomb!"* a woman screamed. A man jumped up in the air and yelled, "Call the police," and the druggist cried, "It's sabotage!" By that time, Dagwood was extracting his son from under the porch railing. He went indoors, and a crowd of determined-looking men, including several policemen, marched into the house and carried the bewildered Dagwood out with them.

"Flip him in the wagon," a policeman directed.

Blondie dashed downtown to buy a new dress and hat, explaining to Alexander, "It's to wear at Daddy's trial."

At the police station, Dagwood explained, "It's not a bomb. It's just a bowling ball."

The disgusted police sergeant said, "Yes, Bumstead, and you don't know how sorry I am I have to let you go free."

The episode ended with Blondie informing him that he owed her sixteen dollars for the new dress and hat, while Alexander danced around delightedly, crying, "Wasn't that fun, Pop? Cops and G-Men and everything!"

It was fun for everyone except Dagwood, and now to make matters worse, he found that the police sergeant still remembered the incident, and still retained the impression that he was sorry to have to let Dagwood go free.

"We might as well forget about trying to get the

He Rolled the Shiny Ball into the Drugstore

police to believe you, Dagwood," Blondie said.

"Maybe they would believe me if I show them the whiskers that I grabbed off that man," her husband said, hopefully.

Blondie shook her head. "Think how that would sound to them, Dagwood. I can just picture you dashing up to the sergeant, saying, 'Here are some whiskers. *Now* do you believe me?' He'd put you in a padded cell so fast you wouldn't know what was happening to you. By the way, let *me* see those whiskers."

Dagwood promptly handed the few strands to her. She put them into an envelope, saying, "Perhaps we can use them later."

"We'll have to find the face they grew on," Dagwood commented.

"That's impossible," Blondie laughed. "They're false."

"False!" Dagwood couldn't believe it, until he had taken them out of the envelope and subjected them to a closer scrutiny. Then he was forced to admit that Blondie was right. The coarse black whiskers that he had pulled from the intruder's beard were undeniably false whiskers.

"Gosh!" he said. "What should we do now?"

Blondie could see that it was up to her to take command of the situation.

"First, we're going to go all through the house to

be certain that our unwanted guest is not here, then
we're going to lock up tight, and then we're going
into the basement again," she declared.

Unhappily, Dagwood agreed to follow her instructions. "What are we going to do down there?"
he wanted to know when they finally finished the
inspection tour of the house and began descending
the basement stairs.

"Take your flashlight and look in all the corners,
including the fruit cellar and coalbin, and all other
possible hiding places," she directed.

"It—it's getting late, Blondie. Don't you think we
ought to go to bed and get up early in the morning to do it?" queried Dagwood.

"I couldn't sleep a wink, and neither could you,
dear, unless we had thoroughly searched the house."
She offered to hold his arm while he investigated,
but he thrust out his chest and waved her aside.
While he searched, Blondie ran upstairs and came
back down carrying the camera.

"Did you find anything suspicious?" she asked
Dagwood.

"Not even a false whisker," he smiled.

Blondie sighed with relief. "Now we can get to
work," she said.

"To work!" Dagwood was aghast. "I thought we
were going to go to bed."

"This won't take very long, Dagwood. But we

simply must get the negatives developed. You ad-
vertised that you had pictures of the accident, remember? We must make sure that you have. We
can't offer to sell something we haven't got."

"But it was a blind ad, Blondie. The people who
want to know about it will write to me using a number. They won't know who I am, and I can take my
time about answering," he glibly explained.

Blondie paid no attention to him, and began
fussing with the developing equipment. Dagwood
shook his head, yawned, and began taking over the
job.

Blondie patted him affectionately.

"Besides that, dear, I'm burning up with curiosity
myself," she confided. "I want to see the new picture of Cookie."

"Okay," Dagwood sighed. "We'll work on that
one first, then we'll do the crash pictures, and then
that is absolutely all. But I'm warning you, that one
of Cookie isn't very good."

"I won't blame you if it isn't," Blondie soothed.
"And I'll stand guard when you turn out the darkroom lights."

The developing solution was already mixed
from the other batch of pictures, and it was not long
before Dagwood finished his task.

"We'd better let them hang until morning before
we touch them," he said.

But Blondie was determined to get a view of the pictures before she went to bed. She took the first wet negative, and held it up to the light.

She laughed. It happened to be the one of Alexander, taken at an angle. The boy was wearing a look of patient resignation.

Then they held up the picture of Cookie. It really didn't look much like Cookie at all.

"Shucks, it's all out of focus," Dagwood complained.

Blondie studied it in silence.

"It isn't a very clear one," she admitted. "The cars in the background are much clearer than the baby."

Dagwood was about to throw it aside, but Blondie retrieved it. Then she looked over his shoulder as he peeked at the other negatives.

"Blondie!" he exclaimed. "Look! I think we can figure out the license number on the car that's leaving the accident!"

Blondie shuddered. She could clearly see the woman at the wheel of the crashed car. The face expressed agony, and pity for the doomed stranger welled up in Blondie's heart. When she turned to Dagwood, there were tears in her eyes. Dagwood was making an effort to keep his eyes open, and his hand pressed to his aching head aroused Blondie's sympathy for him.

"We'll finish in the morning, dear," she said. She insisted that Dagwood go upstairs to bed. Then she made certain that all the basement windows were locked before she followed him.

CHAPTER FIVE

At an early morning hour, which Dagwood complained was the middle of the night, Blondie awakened him, insisting that he get up and continue working on the films.

"It's cruel and inhuman, that's what it is, getting a man up at this hour," he complained.

"But you can go to bed an hour earlier tonight, and come out even," Blondie brightly pointed out.

"Phnnf! What is important enough to make you treat me like this?" Dagwood was about to turn over for another snooze, when something at the foot of the bed attracted his attention. He sat bolt upright in bed.

"What's that?" he demanded.

"That" proved to be the boy puppy, Elmer, who had managed to sneak into the bedroom again, although Dagwood had thrown him out earlier in the night.

"Now you are awake, Dagwood, thanks to little Elmer," Blondie smiled, patting the pup and shooing him out of the room.

"You win," Dagwood yawned, reluctantly reaching for his bathrobe and slippers. Blondie was wearing a satin housecoat with an old rose background, splashed with white gardenia blossoms.

"A lovely, golden-haired girl like you should be sitting still, concentrating on being her beautiful self, instead of pulling sleepy people out of bed," her husband informed her.

Blondie smiled sweetly at him. "Now don't try to flatter me into letting you sleep some more, dear. We simply *must* get the pictures ready, because I feel sure you are going to get a response to your ad in the paper."

She had struck the right note. Dagwood immediately had visions of a big, fat check paying him for all the trouble he had been through. Surprising Blondie with his alacrity, he preceded her to the basement darkroom.

"We might as well throw away the one of Cookie," Dagwood said. "I'll use it for a test print."

When he had it finished, he gave it to Blondie. She studied it closely, then thrust it in front of Dagwood's eyes.

"Take a real good look at it, Dagwood," she said. Dagwood glanced at it again. Then he looked at Blondie, wondering what she had in mind.

"It's a punk picture, if I ever saw one," he commented.

Blondie, instead of agreeing or disagreeing with his opinion, merely asked if she might have the negative. Dagwood gave it to her, along with a questioning glance, then turned back to his work of printing the pictures.

"Oh, boy! Will these pictures be valuable to someone. I've got three views of the car smacked up against that lamppost, and I think you can read the license plate on the car driving away. Look, Blondie!"

Blondie forced herself to look again at the picture of the dying woman in the wrecked car.

"Th—that's an expensive car," she said.

"A limousine, no less. And these pictures should bring limousine prices," Dagwood gloated. The thought of a big check and what he would do with it drifted quickly through his head.

"People certainly gathered around it in a hurry," Blondie said.

"Not us! I took Alexander, Alvin, and Cookie and got away as fast as possible," boasted Dagwood. He scrutinized the snapshots again. "See that woman standing there? She's the one who ran me down and made me drop my camera."

After another minute of study, he pointed at another person. "That looks to me like the fellow in the pin-striped suit who jumped down my throat when I went back. You can't see him very well, because his hat is pulled down."

There was a clatter on the steps. Alexander, Daisy,

and the puppies appeared to inform Dagwood and Blondie that they wanted breakfast. Alexander complained loudly, Daisy barked, and the puppies whined.

"And I suppose Cookie is yowling upstairs," Dagwood sighed.

"Yep," Alexander agreed.

Dagwood hastily thrust the newly-printed snapshots in his print-blotting book, and gave it to Blondie.

"Put that in a good, safe place. Put something heavy on top of it, so the pictures will dry flat and not curl up. We might as well get this hungry mob fed."

Blondie agreed. "And don't forget, you must hurry and get ready to go to the office."

She herded the boy and the dogs upstairs, carrying the blotting book under her arm. Then she searched for a good place to put it. Dagwood had mentioned putting something heavy on top of it, and the heaviest thing she could think of at the moment was the Dutch oven. She put the book on a pantry shelf, and placed the heavy iron kettle on top of it.

Dagwood galloped up the steps at top speed. As he shaved and dressed, he attempted to carry on a conversation with Blondie by shouting down the hall.

Dagwood Shaved and Dressed at Top Speed

"I think I'll try to get the boss to let me off early today. I'll tell him I have an important matter of business which requires my personal attention. I'll tell him—"

"Breakfast is ready," Blondie interrupted. "What's more, you won't tell him anything of the kind. You won't get any answers to your ad until the newspaper is printed. You could stop at the *News* office and see if there are any letters before you come home."

Dagwood opened his mouth, then shut it. Blondie's suggestion was logical and left no room for argument.

"Besides, Dagwood, this is my cleaning day," she added. "I called up the employment agency and told them to send over a cleaning woman. You would just be in our way."

"I've only two minutes to catch my bus," Dagwood lamented, as he tried to gulp down his coffee. It was too hot to drink, so he picked up the cup and ran out in the hall with it.

"What are you doing?" Blondie asked.

"I'm holding it out the door to cool it off," he explained. He drew the cup back into the room, took a big swallow, and then gasped, "Phooey!"

"What's the matter now?" Blondie inquired.

"Why didn't someone tell me it was raining?" he complained.

Blondie held his coat and opened the door for him. There, standing at the door, was a heavy-set woman with a plaid shawl tied around her head.

"Who's that?" Dagwood whispered.

"That must be the cleaning woman," Blondie said in an aside. To the woman, she said, brightly, "Did the employment agency send you here to help with the housework?"

"Me no spik Eenglish. Me scrub," the woman answered. "Wash weendow. Sweep rug. Do dish. Clean good."

Dagwood and Blondie smiled at each other. Then Dagwood suddenly remembered that he would have to sprint after his bus and he swished out the door and down to the bus stop.

Throughout the day, Dagwood had trouble keeping his mind on his work. Puzzling things about the accident continually popped into his mind, and once Mr. Dithers came in to demand why Dagwood had written "Striped Suit" on an invoice for girders.

Questions whirled around his head. Was his imagination playing tricks on him? Had he *really* seen that car pull away? The camera wouldn't lie, would it?

That brought to mind the statement Blondie had made about the camera, when she remarked that the camera continually did favors for them, but might possibly get them into trouble.

Dagwood smiled to himself. This time the little black box had performed a whopping big favor. Just how big he would know as soon as the people involved read the advertisement.

Apparently Blondie was putting in an anxious day, too, for she called him on the telephone in the afternoon.

"Are you all right, Dagwood?" she asked anxiously.

"Am I all right? Of course I'm all right, Blondie. Why shouldn't I be?" he asked, with a laugh.

"It—it's only that I have a queer feeling today. I'm worried, and I don't know exactly why." Blondie wrinkled her brow in a worried frown.

"Did you finish cleaning the house?" Dagwood asked.

"Oh, yes, we finished early. Mrs. Wiskulouski is a gem. She cleaned the house from top to bottom, including straightening up all the drawers in the bureaus and dressers, cupboards and desk, the closets and the basement. You couldn't find a speck of dirt with a fine-tooth comb," Blondie enthused.

"Hmmmn. I don't know as I like having a stranger snoop through all my things," her husband answered, dubiously.

"I just couldn't keep up with her, Dagwood. If I'd shake my head 'no,' she'd shake hers 'yes.' "

"Is she there now?"

"No. And she was awfully funny about it, Dagwood. When I tried to get her address so I could call her again, she couldn't understand me. It was very queer."

"That's too bad, Blondie. But I can't talk to you all afternoon. You know what I told you about personal office calls being frowned upon by Mr. Dithers."

"Good-bye, Dagwood," Blondie said, icily.

"But, dear, don't be mad at me." But his wife had broken the connection. He thought of calling her back, then changed his mind, partially influenced by the scowling presence of Mr. Dithers looming in the doorway.

"Keep your mind on your work, Bumstead," Dithers suggested, dryly.

"Yes, sir," Dagwood responded. He also kept one eye on the clock.

When the time arrived for him to leave, Dagwood cautiously left the building through the rear entrance. He didn't want Mr. Dithers to stop him with overtime work on this night. Striding toward the *News* building, Dagwood had to restrain himself from breaking into a run. He stopped to buy a paper, and quickly turned to the classified advertising section to read the notice he had mailed to the newspaper office.

He found it easily enough at the top of the column marked "Personals."

"Will person or persons interested in obtaining snapshots of the accident at Third Street and Grand Avenue get in touch with writer of this ad. X-34."

Dagwood repeated, "X-34. That's me."

Several people were gathered around the information desk inside the News building. Dagwood patiently waited for attention. When the girl turned to him, he inquired, "Anything there for X-34?"

She sent him to the advertising department, where he identified himself by paying for the ad.

"Are there any answers to my ad?" Dagwood repeated.

"Go back to the information desk and inquire," he was told.

There was nothing in the pigeonhole marked X-34, the information clerk told him. Seeing Dagwood's crestfallen face, she explained that the paper had been on the street only a half hour, and he could hardly expect results that soon.

"How soon can I expect some?" Dagwood queried.

The clerk shrugged. "It depends upon what you're selling and who is buying."

"Oh," Dagwood murmured, feeling sheepish because the clerk's expression plainly said he should have been able to figure that out for himself.

Her expression relaxed, and she mentioned that the information desk would be open all evening if he wanted to call back later.

Dagwood decided that he might just as well go home for dinner. Waiting around downtown would not make the letters come in any faster.

"I'll stop in the bakery and take home a chocolate cake. Everybody likes chocolate cake at home," he thought.

Coming into his home, he found Blondie collapsed in a chair.

"What's the trouble, dear? You look all in," he said.

"It's my own fault. I did something very silly today." She went into the kitchen, and returned holding a three-layer chocolate cake. "I baked a chocolate cake, and the oven made the kitchen so hot I got sick."

"That's too bad, dear," Dagwood sympathized. He headed for the front closet, carrying his box of chocolate cake.

"What have you in that box?" Blondie asked.

Dagwood deposited the box on the closet floor. "Oh . . . er . . . er . . . Just an old pair of shoes," he fibbed.

That explanation satisfied Blondie, who switched the conversation to the subject of the advertisement and the hoped-for responses.

Blondie was disappointed in the lack of replies
too, for Dagwood's sake, but reminded him that
there was plenty of time. She went to the kitchen,
and Dagwood followed her. He was about to kiss
her, when she stopped him.

"Wait, Dagwood. Don't kiss me in the kitchen,"
she said, leading him into the next room. "Here,
this is all right."

"Why can't I kiss you in the kitchen?" he asked,
puzzled.

"Because you always look at the cook-pots to see
what we're having for supper while you're kissing
me," she said, petulantly.

"Who, me?" Dagwood grinned, his arms around
her. He gave her a resounding smack, and they
called the family to dinner.

Blondie spoke again of the woman who had helped her with the cleaning.

"Did she act snoopy? As though she was hunting
for something?" questioned Dagwood.

A thought struck Blondie. She jumped up, went
into the pantry, and lifted the Dutch oven. With a
sigh of relief, she informed Dagwood that the blotting book containing the snapshots was there where
she had placed it.

"Was she in here?" he wanted to know, as he peered around. He replaced the heavy iron kettle on the
blotting book, observing that it completely hid it,.

and that it would be the last place a person hunting snapshots would think to look.

"You're being silly, Dagwood," Blondie said. "She was sent over here by the employment agency. Which reminds me—I could get her address from them."

She disappeared into the other room.

"They aren't open evenings," Dagwood called after her.

"Who?"

"The employment agency."

"I'm not going to call there until morning. I'm going to telephone the *News* office and ask them if there is any mail in the X-34 pigeonhole. I want to know if you got any answers to your ad."

Dagwood and Alexander helped themselves to another big wedge of chocolate cake while they waited for her to make·the call. They were enjoying the dessert immensely, when Blondie dashed back into the kitchen.

"Dagwood!" she cried. "There are several answers to your ad down there."

"Phnnf!" Dagwood exclaimed, gulping the cake. As soon as he could speak intelligibly, he asked, "Who are they from?"

"They don't open your mail, silly. You'll have to call for them."

"Okay! Get my coat. Where's my hat? What time

will the bus be along?" The Bumsteads scurried around, getting Dagwood ready.

Then SWISH!—Dagwood was on his way to the newspaper office.

CHAPTER SIX

SURPRISE LETTERS

The letters clutched in his hand, Dagwood hurried home so that he and Blondie could open them together. He counted them again—five. He had no idea so many insurance people would be interested in his own little snapshots, taken with his faithful old camera, he chuckled to himself. As the bus slowly bumped along, Dagwood was tempted to peek into at least one of them, but he refrained, because he wanted his astute young wife to share the big occasion.

Blondie had put the children and the puppies in their respective sleeping quarters, and awaited Dagwood's return with eagerness. But there was also a trace of fear on her face as she greeted him.

Almost plaintively, she said, "I do hope this will be the end of the whole business, Dagwood. You're the most unlucky person in the world, you know. If there's any trouble stalking around, it picks you to land on first!"

"Trouble? This is Lady Luck pouncing on me, Blondie. Look at all the letters!" He gaily waved them at her, and gave them to her to hold while he took off his hat and coat.

Then he whispered, after furtively looking around, "Where are the pictures?"

"Under the watcha-ma-call-it," she whispered back.

Then she laughed. "Why are we whispering?" she said. "There's no one here besides us."

"I don't know why, Blondie. I just felt as though I should whisper."

"I know just how you feel, Dagwood—sort of suspicious. And I don't like the feeling. I don't want things to happen to us, Dagwood. I would rather have our little home running smoothly . . ."

"And efficiently," Dagwood added, with a nod. "But we're in this accident business now. It wasn't my fault that it happened under my nose, was it?"

Blondie agreed that it was just one of those things. "But they always happen to you," she said.

Dagwood picked one of the letters. "Shall we start opening them?"

"That's a splendid idea. We certainly don't want to wait until morning—or perhaps we should."

"Oh, no. Here, I'll open the first one, and you can open the second. We can read them aloud to each other."

This arrangement was agreeable to Blondie. First Dagwood examined the outside of the envelope, commenting that it was from the Acme Company, but he'd never heard of an insurance firm with that

Dagwood Picked Up the Letters

name.

"I'm all ready to read it," he said brightly, in the manner of one about to recite poetry.

" 'X-34

Dear Sir:

In response to your advertisement men-tioning snapshots, we wish to point out that for real service and excellent workmanship in the developing and printing of your films, nowhere in this vicinity will you find the peer of the Acme Photograph Company.

We use only the most modern, scientific methods of producing . . .' "

Dagwood paused in disgust. Blondie suppressed a giggle.

"Enterprising, aren't they?" she remarked.

"Do you want to hear the rest of it?" Dagwood wanted to know.

"Of course not. We'll open mine. It might be a good idea to save that address, though, Dagwood, if the time ever comes when you want real service and excellent workmanship . . ."

"Phooey," Dagwood said, tossing the unwelcome letter into the wastebasket. "You read your letter, Blondie."

The envelope carried the return address of the newspaper. "Are they sending a bill already?"

Blondie wondered.

"They'd better not. I paid for the ad this afternoon."

"What do you suppose they want?"

Dagwood was trying his best to be patient, but could no longer restrain himself.

"For gosh sake, *open it*," he said.

Blondie opened it, and began reading:

" 'X-34:

If your pictures of the Billingate accident are any good we are willing to pay our usual rate of from three to five dollars apiece for them. However, we reserve the right to use or discard them at our own discretion.

Pete Howard
Police Reporter
The News.' "

When she finished reading, Blondie looked very pleased.

"Now that's real nice of them, don't you think?"

Dagwood was indignant. "Three to five dollars! Do they think I'm crazy? Why these pictures are worth a lot more than that! I'll betcha they're worth a fortune!"

"Nonsense, Dagwood," Blondie scoffed. "After all, it only cost you about fifteen cents to make them. Subtract fifteen cents from three dollars each, and you have . . ."

"Never mind that, Blondie. You might as well throw that one in the wastebasket, too. We'll get on with the rest of them."

Blondie wanted to save the letter from the newspaper. "We might have to accept their offer whether we want to or not," she insisted. "I'm not going to throw it away." She carefully placed the letter in the drawer of the desk, and suggested that Dagwood open the next one.

His face lit up with a flashing, triumphant smile. "At last we're getting some *real* results. This one is from the Perpetual Life Casualty Company. Get ready to gasp, Blondie. This is sure to be a man-sized offer, and not a stingy three-dollar bid. Listen to this:

'To Whom It May Concern:

Our firm is handling the insurance details in connection with the accident which occurred at Third Street and Grand Avenue late yesterday afternoon, in which Mrs. Rufus Tyvand Billingate was fatally injured.

Should the pictures you possess interest our company, we would be willing to purchase them. We might add that we sometimes pay as high as twenty-five dollars for pictures of this type.

We would be pleased to have you con-
tact us at your earliest convenience.' "

"I still like the idea of having them published in
the paper," Blondie remarked. Dagwood was astonished to find her unimpressed by the insurance
company's offer.

"This is what I've been hoping for!" he expostu-
lated, crestfallen.

Blondie shrugged. "Then you probably won't
want to bother about opening the next letter."

"Gosh, that's right! I'd forgotten there were some
more. I wonder who sent that one?"

Blondie scrutinized the plain, square envelope.
Neatly printed in the center was "X-34." She pointed out to Dagwood that the stationery was of the
highest quality. As she went into a long dissertation
on the merits of various types of writing paper, Dagwood interrupted with the plea that she read the
letter.

"This is quite a long letter. Perhaps you'd better
read it, Dagwood. You can read it to yourself, and
tell me the highlights. And if it isn't important, I
won't have to listen to any of it."

Dagwood scratched his head, studying Blondie in
a manner which indicated that women are a puzzling
species. Sweet, personable, and pretty as the best of
them, Blondie could sometimes be mighty aggravat-
ing, her husband informed her.

"You were as enthusiastic as possible at first, Blondie, and now you're trying to be indifferent. What changed your mind?"

Blondie admitted that she had changed in her attitude toward making money on the snapshots. She couldn't explain why.

"It's just that—well—we would be better off if we washed our hands of the entire affair."

Dagwood racked his brains in vain for an answer to that reasoning. He began to read the letter to himself, then excitedly started again, reading aloud.

"Listen to this, Blondie!

'Dear Sir or Madam:

The message which you so thoughtfully inserted in this evening's newspaper sounds like the answer to a fervent hope, the desire to get in touch with someone with evidence of the fateful happening of yesterday.' "

Dagwood paused to comment, "Isn't that a good start?"

"Flowery, isn't it?" Blondie responded. "Read on. You can omit the oratorical tone, Dagwood."

Dagwood grumbled something about not being sarcastic, and turned to the letter again.

" 'It is gratifying to know that in this world of struggle and strife, one person would have the cool-headedness to keep

his wits about him at a time of extreme
emergency.' "

Dagwood paused again to announce, "That's
me!"

"Sounds like someone trying to talk you into
giving them to him." Blondie said.

"That's where you're wrong, dear," her husband
was pleased to inform her. "Here's the part that
gets interesting:

'Your pictures are no doubt of inestim-
able value.' "

"How much is that in dollars and cents?" Blondie
inquired, sweetly.

"I'm coming to that part," Dagwood muttered.

" 'In fact, if they are actual views taken at
the scene of the accident, as your advertisement indicates, they might prove to be
worth a considerable sum, and that means
possibly a three-figure amount.' "

Dagwood grinned broadly. "See? Three figures—
that means a hundred or hundreds."

"Then why doesn't he say so?" Blondie demanded.

"He did. That's the way we businessmen talk. We
lay our cards on the table in a very subtle way."

"I prefer the way that police reporter puts his on
the table."

Dagwood was becoming exasperated. "You find

fault with this person and you don't even know who he is."

"Do you?" Blondie demanded.

"Not yet. But I haven't finished reading the letter. Let's see, where did I stop?

'. . . possibly a three-figure amount. However, if negotiations are to proceed, there are certain stipulations which you will be expected to adhere to.' "

"I don't like the sound of that, Dagwood," Blondie said somewhat fearfully.

Ignoring her, Dagwood continued.

" 'First, it is assumed that the entire proceedings will be held in strictest confidence, for if too many outsiders are involved, it would undoubtedly prove both annoying and inconvenient.' "

"That doesn't make sense to me," Blondie interrupted. "Why all this beating around the bush? Why doesn't he or she or they tell you the price they want to pay and tell you where to deliver them and be done with it?"

Dagwood was too busy scanning the remainder of the message to pay attention to her question.

" 'Second, you will, of course, be expected to turn over not only the negatives but all prints which you have made or have had made, together with a signed statement that they are the only views of the accident which you possess.

This statement and any payment of money will necessarily need to be made in the presence of witnesses. You are assured that the sum to be paid will make it well worth your while to agree to these simple, logical stipulations.

As your name and whereabouts are unknown, please be at the corner of Third Street and Grand Avenue, scene of the accident, at five o'clock tomorrow afternoon. A taxi will pick you up and bring you to Brentwood Manor. You will wear a red flower in your lapel for purposes of identification.' "

There was a dramatic pause, while Dagwood waited for the significance of the letter to impress Blondie. Her expression, with a tiny scowl between her pretty eyes. was a signal that she was giving the matter some deep thought. Suddenly, she snapped out of her thinking trance to abruptly ask, "Who signed it?"

Dagwood glanced again at the bottom of the letter, turned it over, referred again to the first page, turned that over, held both sheets up to the light, and then reported, "Nobody!"

Instead of demanding a reason for that, Blondie

waited for Dagwood to think up one. He did.

"Naturally, Blondie," he said, "if I wouldn't give my name in the advertisement, the man with all that money to hand out isn't going to give his."

"All the others gave their names," Blondie retorted. "The Acme Photograph Company, the police reporter, and the insurance company. And I opened the last letter. It's from another insurance company, with the same kind of offer as the other one made. It is also signed."

Dagwood referred again to the two-page message he was holding. "Brentwood Manor. Brentwood Manor," he repeated thoughtfully. "Isn't that where the woman in the car lived?"

"I thought she lived in Shorecrest Park."

"Wasn't it Brentwood Manor, Shorecrest Park?"

"That sounds something like it. Let's look in tonight's paper. There must be more news about the accident," Blondie suggested.

Finding no mention of the accident on the front page, Dagwood turned to the local section. Under the column, "Happenings in the City," he found a small item, and read it to Blondie.

" 'Medical report on the crash that proved fatal to Mrs. Rufus Tyvand Billingate indicates that death was due to a heart attack as the result of shock, rather than to injuries sustained from the impact against the lamppost. Although Mrs. Billingate

Dagwood Read the Article to Blondie

led rather a secluded life, neighbors said she employ-
ed a chauffeur and seldom drove her automobile herself, possibly because she was aware of her heart condition, they surmise. Coroner M. E. Rollins has
called an inquest for Thursday for further investigation.' "

When he had finished reading the article, Dagwood commented that it failed to mention the address.

"Thursday," Blondie mused. "That's the day
after tomorrow, Dagwood. Has it occurred to you,
dear, that you are an important witness in this case?
All you are thinking about is how much money you
can get for your pictures."

Dagwood looked hurt. "That isn't all I think
about, Blondie. Don't forget, I tried to telephone
to the police. Besides, if it is the woman's *family* that
I'm dealing with, I can tell them all about it when
I give them the pictures. By the way, where is last
night's paper? That will have the address in it, and
we can be sure about where this letter came from."

· The newspaper was not in the magazine rack.
Neither could it be found among the papers stacked
in the basement.

"Dear me," Blondie complained. "It was probably at the top of the pile, and was used first."

"Think hard. Blondie," Dagwood said. "What
could you have used it for?"

"I remember, now. Mrs. Wiskulouski insisted on cleaning out all the drawers. We lined some of them with newspapers."

Dagwood groaned. "Does that mean we've got to empty all of them?"

Blondie assured him that they would probably find the missing front page at the bottom of one of the first drawers they emptied. But she was over-optimistic. They searched in all the drawers in all the furniture downstairs, then climbed the stairs.

"We'll have to turn on the light in the children's room," Blondie said, with regret. Luckily, Alexander and Cookie were too lost in slumber to be disturbed. The hunt through their bureau, however, proved fruitless. Dagwood and Blondie, after a fond glance at the sleeping children, tiptoed downstairs again.

A slight sound behind Dagwood caused him to whisper, "What's that?"

Blondie giggled. "It's Daisy's little boy puppy, Elmer. He doesn't want to miss anything."

"Go back to bed, Elmer," Dagwood ordered. "We still haven't found that paper, Blondie."

Shaking her head, Blondie tried to recall what possibly could have happened to it. She spied a tiny swirl of dust on the floor, and stooped to pick it up. It proved an inspiration. "I think I know where it is, Dagwood!" she cried. "I remember now! We

emptied the vacuum cleaner bag on a sheet of newspaper."

"Couldn't you have thought of that before?" asked the disgruntled Dagwood. He knew what he
would have to do—go out in the back yard with his
flashlight and get the package of sweepings out of
the garbage container. Blondie made him put on his
coat and hat.

He was spotlighting the garbage can in the back
yard with his flashlight, when a voice from a window
in the next house shouted, "Who's there?"

Dagwood recognized the voice as that of Woodley.
"It's me, Bumstead!" he called back, as he lifted the
cover of the garbage can, and reached for the top
bundle. He knew by the size that it was the right
one, for he recalled the time he had sent such a
package over to Woodley. He had grabbed the
wrong bundle and sent the dust, neatly wrapped. A
short time later, a messenger boy had rung the doorbell and handed a box to Dagwood. "What a sense
of humor!" he had exclaimed, when he found that it
contained the Bumstead's sweepings, direct from
Woodley.

Apparently, Woodley recalled the same incident.
"I hope you aren't thinking up any cute tricks,
Bumstead!" he called. "What are you doing down
there, anyway?"

Quick as a wink, Dagwood replied, "I'm looking

He Looked in the Garbage Can

for Elmer."

"In the garbage can?" Woodley was incredulous.

There was a tiny barking sound in the stillness of the night. Dagwood turned his flashlight toward his feet, and there, indeed, was Elmer.

"You can go back to sleep, Woodley," Dagwood chuckled. "I found him."

The window slammed, and Dagwood carried the puppy and the package into the house, where Blondie spread more papers on the floor and emptied the dirt from the important newspaper.

At last they had found the front page of the paper!

Dagwood held it up triumphantly—and then his eyes widened. There was a hole on the first page, made by a careful clipping of the item concerning the Billingate accident.

Her mouth open in amazement, Blondie quickly denied having cut out the story.

"Well, I didn't!" Dagwood complained. "Someone did it. It certainly wouldn't be torn out by accident with carefully squared corners!"

"Stop shouting, Dagwood!" Blondie begged. "We can find another paper, or buy one downtown tomorrow."

Puzzled and bewildered, Dagwood scratched his head. "Who could have done that? Were there any people in the house today?"

"No one besides Mrs. Wiskulouski. And she can't talk English, remember?"

"But can she *read* it?"

"If she can't talk it, she certainly can't read it," Blondie replied. Then she murmured, so softly that her words were not discernible to Dagwood, "*If* she can't talk it."

CHAPTER SEVEN

TWO PASSENGERS

After retiring for the night, Dagwood followed his usual custom of getting up again to make a sandwich. Sandwiches to him were not mere slabs of bread with a slice of something separating them. Dagwood's sandwiches were a work of Bumstead art.

The sandwich artist assembled one of his specialties, murmuring, "Let's see—cole slaw, beans, sardines, cheese, mayonnaise, piccalilli—"

He surveyed the tower of food proudly, then with one hand on the bottom and the other on the top, he made his way back to the bedroom.

As he opened his mouth to its greatest extent, ready to sink his teeth in his tidbit, Blondie sat up in bed and said, "Darling, there's a big mosquito flying around in here."

Dagwood's quick glance darted around the wall. He spied the mosquito. He tossed the handiest thing at it—his six-layer sandwich, which landed with a loud "SPLAT!" as it scattered moist food all over the room.

"I got him! I got him!" he shouted in triumph, until he noticed the look of abject horror on Blondie's face. Meekly, the man of the house descended the stairs in search of broom and dustpan.

"I got excited," he explained, as he stooped down and ruefully gathered the cole slaw, beans, sardines, cheese, mayonnaise, and piccalilli together in the dustpan.

"Clean it up and don't talk so much," his wife snapped.

That was not the only trouble that interrupted Dagwood's sleep that night. When all was quiet and serene, the baby awakened and began to cry. Her father tried to soothe her by singing, but she voiced loud objections. He picked her up from her crib, and began pacing the floor.

"Please stop crying, Cookie," he pleaded. Then he had an idea. He knew how to make her stop yelling. He took her downstairs.

Not long afterward Blondie called, "Dagwood, why are you running the vacuum at two a. m.?"

"Cookie likes it. It's the only thing that will keep her quiet."

"B-z-z-z," the vacuum hummed.

"I gotta get some sleep!" Dagwood said. He carried Cookie and the vacuum upstairs. "I'll plug it in up here and put her in her crib," he decided.

The idea worked as far as quieting Cookie's crying was concerned, but the "B-z-z-z-z" of the vacuum kept Dagwood awake. He was grateful when Cookie finally fell asleep and he could unplug the cleaner.

Then the mosquito, which apparently had dodged the well-aimed sandwich, buzzed around the room. Determinedly, Dagwood grasped a fly swatter and went after it. Taking careful aim, he whammed the weapon against the wall.

"Ah—I got it! Thank goodness, now I can go to sleep and get my rest," he said.

"W-a-a-a!" Cookie began her midnight concert.

"Now, you woke the baby!" Blondie admonished.

Dagwood picked up his child again, and began pacing the floor, complaining, "All nature is against me!"

Dagwood paced toward the front door, for the bell was ringing. He wondered who could be calling on the Bumsteads at that late hour. Someone about the pictures of the accident, perhaps. But it was just his next door neighbor, Herb Woodley.

"How do you expect a man to sleep with your baby yelling like that?" Woodley shouted, shaking his fist.

Dagwood was in no mood to be congenial. "If you think you can do better, come in and try to put her to sleep yourself," he retorted.

Woodley took the baby from him and began walking up and down.

"Try jiggling her," Dagwood suggested.

"Shut up and go and see who's ringing your doorbell," was the curt rejoinder.

"How Do You Expect a Man to Sleep?"
Woodley Shouted

It was another irate neighbor demanding to know
how he was expected to sleep. Dagwood and Herb
invited him to come in and have a try. The three
men formed a walking brigade, Woodley and Bumstead following their neighbor, who was carrying
Cookie.

"Try singing," Dagwood said.

"Yeah, try a lullaby," Herb Woodley added.

"Pipe down. I've got her to sleep," they were told.
Carefully, Cookie was lowered into her crib. Dagwood took his midnight guests to the door, calling
after them, "Thanks, boys!"

What little remained of the night was spent in
comparative quiet. At any rate, no more prowlers
with whiskers paid a visit to the busy Bumstead
home.

The next morning was bright, but Dagwood
wasn't. He sat up, his eyes heavy-lidded, and decided
he might as well start the day with a nice, warm
bath while Blondie prepared his breakfast.

He scrubbed himself in a hurry.

"*Blondie!* Phone the plumber to come over. The
bathwater won't run down the drain," he bellowed.
Instead of telephoning, Blondie came upstairs to
investigate.

"There's nothing the matter. You left the wash-
rag in the tub and it covered the drain," she said.
Then she confronted Dagwood with her hand ex-

tended. "Now give me the money you would have paid the plumber."

Dagwood jollied her out of that request, and began to shave. Alexander's voice was the next one heard.

"*Papa—quick!* Mama's caught in the folding ironing board and can't get up," the boy shouted.

"Oh, my goodness," Dagwood exclaimed, rapidly wielding his razor.

Alexander rushed into the bathroom.

"Didn't you hear me? Quick! Mama's caught in the folding ironing board," he shouted.

"I heard you," Dagwood said impatiently. "I'm shaving as fast as I can!"

But the indignant Blondie had extricated herself from the ironing board trap by that time. It was too close to time for Dagwood's departure for her to scold him. Instead, she talked about Dagwood's plans for the day.

"Have you decided what to do about the pictures?" she asked.

"Decided! There's nothing to decide! Naturally, I'm going to meet the taxi at Third and Grand this afternoon."

"Aren't you going to acknowledge the other letters?"

"Nope! The man said it was in confidence."

Blondie could quickly see that her husband was

in no mood to quibble after his bad night. Plainly
troubled, she regarded him in silence for a few moments before broaching the subject uppermost on
her mind.

"Wouldn't it be advisable to talk to the newspaper reporter. Dagwood?"

"Later, maybe," he conceded. "If there is something fishy about my correspondent, you can leave
it to me to discover it at once."

The look his wife gave him indicated that she
wasn't as sure of his character-discovering ability as
he. But she maintained silence, preferring to keep
from vexing him any further.

"You might stop at the newspaper office to see if
you have more letters," she suggested. "You are coming home before you meet this person, aren't you?"

"Certainly. I'll come home early and maybe we
can have an early dinner. But remember, I must be
at the corner at five o'clock."

They had spent too much time talking, the clock
revealed, and Dagwood had to dash out the door and
sprint down the street to catch his bus He barely
got there. and the conductor, who helped haul Dagwood aboard, sighed, "I wish we could get you up
two minutes earlier mornings!"

Mr. Dithers reluctantly agreed to allow Dagwood
to leave early on the condition that he get all of

his work out before he left. That left Dagwood little time to eat his lunch, and no time at all to go to the *News* office. He sent the office boy to see if there were more letters, and was surprised to find that there were three of them.

"A man stopped me and asked me if I was 'X-34,' " the boy reported.

That interested Dagwood. "What did you say, and what did he look like?" he questioned.

"I told him 'nope,' " the boy answered. "He looked like someone who worked there, because he came out of the room marked 'Editorial.' "

"Oho!" Dagwood remarked. "That must be the police reporter."

"Then he went over to talk to the girl at the information desk and I skipped out."

"Okay. Buy yourself a soda," Dagwood grinned, slipping a quarter into the boy's hand. He returned to his desk to examine the letters. Blondie could see them later, but he was anxious to find out immediately whether there was another message from the person who was planning to have the taxicab pick him up. The first was another blurb from the photo-finishing firm, which Dagwood tossed aside with a snort of disdain. The second letter was from the Perpetual Insurance Company. This he tucked into an inner pocket of his coat. The third he read with considerable interest. It was another note from Pete

Howard, the police reporter of the *News*.

X-34: This is final notice about your pictures. They won't be any good to us . after the inquest. If you have another prospective buyer, there's no law stopping you from selling extra prints, is there? If you think there is, see me, and we'll look it up.

"He's a slicker," Dagwood said, to no one in particular.

"Yes, sir," the office boy obligingly answered.

"Dog-gone! I'm tempted to go to see him." He toyed with the idea for awhile, then happened to glance at the clock. It was almost time for him to leave, and he wouldn't have time now. The office boy's freckled face showed his curiosity, but Dagwood gave him no information.

He lost no time in leaving the office, thankful that he had finished his day's work.

"*Yoo-hoo*, I'm home," Dagwood called, as he entered the Bumsteads' front hallway.

He marched into the kitchen, grabbed his pretty wife, and kissed her with a loud smack.

"Gee, it was sweet of you to kiss me before you looked in the cook-pot to see what we're going to have for supper," Blondie smiled, thrilled and pleased at his devotion.

Tactlessly, Dagwood explained, "I didn't have to

look—I could smell the ham and cabbage in the hall."

Blondie sighed and smiled and asked about the letters, and added that she had an incident she wanted to relate to him. And there was so little time.

"We can talk while we eat," she said.

"You always tell me *not* to talk when I'm eating," Alexander reminded his mother.

"I mean *you* shouldn't talk with your mouth full of food, dear," Blondie said.

"Is there a difference?" queried Alexander.

Blondie nodded. "But I can't take time to explain it to you, now."

Dagwood cautioned, "Just remember to keep quiet, Alexander, while your mother and father are talking over a serious matter."

Alexander was not exactly overjoyed at the prospect of being a silent guest at the meal, because he had a lot of things to talk about, too. He soon forgot about his peevishness when Blondie set a big dish of ham and cabbage before him. He was too busy with his dinner to take more than a passing interest in the conversation between his parents.

"Tell me about the letters, first," Blondie said.

Dagwood explained, with a laugh, the "follow-up" advertising letter from the photography firm. "I filed that one in the nearest wastebasket."

"And the others?"

After reaching inside his coat, Dagwood produced the one from the insurance firm. He hesitated a moment or two before handing her the note from the police reporter. He anticipated what her reaction would be, and found he was correct.

"Oh, Dagwood, you should have stopped in to see him!"

"I thought of it, dear, but there wasn't time. I'll see him tonight if I get back in time, otherwise I can get in touch with him first thing in the morning. It isn't because I want to make any more money than what I'm offered in the Brentwood Manor letter, but I would just as soon do a favor for the newspaper. There might come a day when I'll want them to do a favor for me. I think I'll be a holdout—and not close the deal with anyone until I've looked at it from all angles," Dagwood said, punctuating his remarks by smacking his left hand with his right fist.

"That's sensible," Blondie admitted "But you must hurry and finish your dinner. Then I'll tell you something. You can keep right on eating while I talk."

His mouth stuffed with food, Dagwood nodded.

While pouring coffee for him, Blondie told about a telephone call she had made during the day.

"That foreign woman, Mrs. Wiskulouski, was such a good worker that I wanted to be sure not to lose track of her. I wanted to tell the employment bureau to send her here when I needed help.

"When I called them and asked for her telephone number, guess what they told me, Dagwood?"

"Glub, glub," was the only response Dagwood could make with his mouth stuffed with food, which sent Alexander into gales of appreciative laughter.

"Quiet, son," Blondie admonished "Well, Dagwood, the people at the employment bureau told me that they had no such person on their list of workers. They said that the woman they sent over here yesterday was named Swenson."

"They were probably mixed up," Dagwood said. "We sometimes get mixed up on names at the Dithers Construction Company, too. If I were you, I wouldn't worry about it."

"But that isn't all, Dagwood They said Mrs. Swenson came back and said that I turned her back, saying I didn't need her They seemed quite put out about it!"

"Ha ha!" Dagwood laughed. "Mrs. Wiskulouski probably overheard them telling Mrs. Swenson to come here, and got here first, and then answered the door and turned her away."

"That sounds simple," Blondie agreed, "except that Mrs. Wiskulouski can't understand or talk the English language very well. I had to draw pictures for her."

Dagwood brushed the matter aside. "She cleaned

the house, and you can forget about her."

"I wish I could," Blondie responded.

"Mrs. Swenson will probably turn out to be a better cleaning woman than Mrs. Wiskulouski," Dagwood soothed. He jumped to his feet, exclaiming that it was high time he was leaving for his appointment at Third Street and Grand Avenue.

"You have fifteen minutes to spare, and it only takes two minutes to get to the corner," Blondie said, trying to quiet Dagwood's impatience.

Nervously, Dagwood rubbed his hand over his chin. "I—I hope everything will be all right," he said.

"I—I hope so, too," Blondie said, worriedly She put a restraining hand on Dagwood's arm. "Are you sure you want to go there, dear?"

There was a slight hesitation, then Dagwood squared his shoulders. "Of course I'm sure. Where are my hat and coat?"

Alexander asked, innocently, "Aren't they in the closet where you always put them?"

"Hush, Alexander. Papa is being dramatic," Blondie chided.

While she helped Dagwood with his coat, a thought struck her.

"Alexander, ask Mrs. Woodley if she has time to come over here and stay with you for about ten minutes, will you?"

Dagwood Waited Impatiently for Time to Leave

"Okay, Mom," Alexander said, darting out the back door.

"What for? Where are you going?" Dagwood wanted to know.

"I'm going to walk to the corner with you, Dagwood. You're too nervous to stand there all by yourself."

"That's silly, Blondie. The way you treat me, you'd think I was a two-year-old."

"That's because you sometimes act like one," she replied. "Have you forgotten anything?"

"I don't think so."

"Ha!" she said, triumphantly. "See what I mean? You haven't the films and prints, and you haven't the red flower in your buttonhole."

"Oh, gosh!" Dagwood groaned. He began to run around, waving his arms.

"Keep calm, dear," Blondie suggested. "You go into the other room and get a red flower from my artificial bouquet on the round table, and I'll get the pictures and films from under the Dutch oven. I'll be back in a minute."

Time was getting short. As Blondie thrust the films and snapshots into his hand, Dagwood frantically asked, "Are you sure they are all here? Did you get them all?"

"All of the accident pictures are there. They don't want a picture of Cookie or the puppies at a picnic, do they?"

"Don't be funny at a time like this," Dagwood wailed. "Of course not!" In the midst of the hub-bub, which included excited yelping by Daisy and the pups, whooping by Alexander, who was always ready to get into the spirit of anything, and gurgling by Cookie, who banged on her high-chair tray, Mrs. Woodley came into the kitchen.

"Will you watch them for a few minutes?" Blondie asked.

"I can if you will be back within an hour," Mrs. Woodley told her.

"If I can't, I'll send someone over to relieve you. But I don't think I'll be gone more than—" she glanced at the clock—"eight minutes. Hurry, Dagwood!"

The two of them ran out, leaving Mrs. Woodley staring after them in a puzzled fashion but, knowing the Bumsteads, she expected that anything might happen.

Blondie took two steps to every one of Dagwood's as they hurried down the street. They almost bump-ed into a woman wearing a plaid shawl over her head.

"Was—wasn't that Mrs. Wiskulouski?" Blondie panted.

"I don't know, Blondie, and we haven't time to find out. You can try to catch up with her if you want to. I can find Third and Grand by myself, you know."

But Blondie kept her hand tucked beneath Dagwood's elbow, as she tried to keep up with his man-sized stride.

No cars were in sight when they reached the designated corner.

"Are you sure it was Third and Grand?" Dagwood wondered. peering up and down the streets but seeing nothing.

"That's what the note said. Perhaps it's too late." There was a hopeful note in Blondie's voice. She did not want Dagwood to go.

"We'll wait awhile and find out."

Neither could think of anything to say. A truck rumbled past, going down Third Street. A sport roadster turned onto Grand Avenue. Blondie and Dagwood watched them while they disappeared from view.

"Let's go back home," Blondie coaxed.

Dagwood patted her hand, and sighed. Then he straightened.

"Look!" He pointed toward an alley entrance halfway down Third Street. An orange-colored taxicab was parked there.

"Did you notice that there before?" Blondie whispered.

"N-No," Dagwood said, his voice trembling with

nervousness. "It—it just sort of popped up. Do you suppose he's waiting for you to go away?"

"If he is, he has a long wait!" Blondie said firmly, folding her arms and tapping one foot. Dagwood knew it was useless to try to send her home when she took that attitude. It would be like trying to budge a brick wall.

They waited, neither saying a word. And the taxicab continued to park in the alley entrance.

"We can outwait him," Blondie said.

The taxicab, after a minute or two, began to move.

"Here he comes," Dagwood said.

But he was mistaken. The cab moved away from them, instead of toward them.

"I guess he gave up," Dagwood said.

"Do I hear a note of relief in Mr. Bumstead's voice?" Blondie asked.

"W-Well," he began, then halted, pointing down Grand Avenue. "Here he comes again. He must have decided to go around the block."

Blondie clutched Dagwood's arm, as the taxicab slowed up, and stopped in front of them. The driver reached back and opened the door.

Before Dagwood could stop her, Blondie darted into the rear of the cab. Astounded, Dagwood followed her.

The driver turned. "But, lady, I was only supposed to haul one fare," he declared.

"Like it or not, you're hauling two," Blondie said decisively.

The driver shrugged, and drove ahead.

CHAPTER EIGHT

A CHILLY WELCOME

Dagwood knew better than to argue with his determined young wife, as she sat straight, with her arms folded across her chest, and her eyes staring at the back of the cab-driver's neck. The driver turned once more to say something, took one look at Blondie, another at Dagwood, shrugged and turned his attention exclusively to driving.

"Brentwood Manor is within walking distance of our house," Blondie told Dagwood in an undertone. "I looked it up today, on a map of the city. If everything seems to be going along as it should, I can walk home from there. Or I can wait for you, and we can walk home together."

"You told Mrs. Woodley you'd be gone only a few minutes," Dagwood chided.

"The conference should be all over within an hour," Blondie insisted. "And she mentioned that she could stay that long." She paused. "Do you mean to tell me that you don't *want* me to go with you?"

That was putting Dagwood in a quandary. He did and he didn't want to have her with him, and he groped for words to express his attitude.

"It's hard to explain, dear. I want to have you

with me because you think clearly and quickly. If these people are trying to pull any tricks, you would know it. *But,* I'm the one that is to blame for whatever happens, and I don't want to drag you into it. You were suspicious of the letter, remember?"

"That's very sweet of you, Dagwood. But whatever you're mixed up in is my worry, too. You're our papa bird with ten little mouths to feed," she reminded him.

The taxicab was slowing down. The Bumsteads immediately became interested in the part of town through which they were being driven.

"That must be the place," Blondie whispered.

"You can't see much of it," Dagwood commented.

In the exclusive residential district through which they were traveling, the estate with the metal scrollwork lettering "Brentwood Manor" above a big iron gate was unique in that it was entirely surrounded by a high wall of mottled stone. On top of the wall, sharp iron pickets further emphasized the keep-out atmosphere of the property. A few old trees and the gabled roof of the huge brick mansion towered into view beyond the wall which ran the length of a city block in two directions from the heavy iron gate.

"It—it looks sort of menacing, doesn't it?" Blondie quavered.

"Don't be silly, Blondie. These people are very

exclusive. You can tell by that how rich they are. We don't have to build high walls around our house. But if we were millionaires, we would have to take some precautions if we wanted to keep on being millionaires. People are always trying to steal things from and sell things to millionaires."

Blondie giggled nervously. "Someone tried to steal your films, and book agents are always trying to sell you books. Does that make *you* a millionaire?"

Dagwood was about to go into a long explanation, when he saw that she was merely teasing him. The taxi stopped, facing the gate.

"Pretty classy, visiting prominent people," Dagwood beamed. "Nothing too good for the Bumsteads."

Loud tooting from the taxi horn drowned him out. After an interval of silent waiting, a man wearing a butler's suit appeared on the other side of the gate. Instead of opening the big double gate, he unlocked a smaller section, about the size of a house door at one side of it.

"I can't get through that," said the cab driver. "This ain't no undersize jeep. Looks like this is where you folks get out."

Blondie and Dagwood looked questioningly at each other, then emerged from the cab.

"Perhaps madame would wish the automobile retained for her return?" the man at the gate inquired in nasal tones.

"No, thank you," Blondie answered politely, quickly stepping through the entrance. Dagwood followed her. They waited while the butler paid the cabby, and then docilely followed as he haughtily led them down the long, brick walk leading to the huge, square mansion.

"I've seen that butler somewhere," Dagwood muttered.

"He keeps his nose so high up in the air, and with his eyes half closed you can't tell what he looks like," Blondie said. "I don't think he's very happy about me."

"I'm happy about you," Dagwood said. "But I wish you were home. Did you hear the gate lock snap shut? I don't think I'd like being so exclusive," Dagwood said.

Blondie tugged at his arm. "Let's run back," she urged.

"Sh-sh! We can't now. Look at that house! Did you ever see such elaborate pillars?"

The butler was walking as fast as his dignity would permit, and the Bumsteads quickly surveyed the exterior of Brentwood Manor. It was built of brick yellowed with age, and the pillars, cupolas, and elaborate trim were painted white. The ornate grillwork and stone steps of the wide veranda showed that no expense had been spared to make the structure one

They Followed the Butler Up the Drive

of the showplaces of its day.

"It's too elaborate to suit me," Blondie said.

"They were all elaborate when this was built," Dagwood reminded her.

"I'll bet it has a big barn in the back, with servant's quarters upstairs," Blondie surmised.

"Probably a garage, now," Dagwood said. "I'm more worried about the *inside* of the place than I am about the outside."

"What do you mean by that remark, Dagwood? Let's not go in at all, if you feel that way about it."

"You don't understand, Blondie. I'm nervous about talking to whoever wrote that letter. How do I know what kind of person he might turn out to be? He didn't sign his name, and he didn't open the gate. Why should we have to walk up to the building? There's a special covered entryway for cars to drive under on the side," Dagwood observed.

Blondie was about to remind Dagwood that *she* had been suspicious of the letter, but she said, instead, "There's no law to make you do business with this stranger, Dagwood. The best thing to do is to listen to what he has to say, tell him you'll think it over, and then go home and we'll talk about it."

They followed the butler up the steps and across the porch. They waited while he unlocked the huge, carved door. Involuntarily both Dagwood and Blondie hesitated as he opened the door and waited for them to step inside. Then Blondie took a deep breath and walked in. Dagwood followed closely.

The tapestried entrance hall with its huge crystal chandelier overwhelmed the Bumsteads with its showiness. A thick oriental rug, gold-framed oil paintings, and rich damask furniture in the drawing room were taken in with a sweeping glance by the observant Blondie as she and Dagwood were ushered into the room.

"Your cards?" the butler inquired in an undertone.

Flustered, Blondie hurriedly explained that she hadn't even brought her purse with her.

"Have you any calling cards with you, Dagwood?" she whispered.

"Only Dithers Construction Company cards," he informed her. He held one out to the butler, who eyed it with disdain.

"There's some mistake," he said. "This is not your card."

Blondie was quick to ask, "How did *you* know?" but her question was ignored as the aloof servant turned his attention to Dagwood.

"That's my boss's card," Dagwood laughed. "My name's Bumstead—Dagwood Bumstead. And this is Mrs. Bumstead—Mrs. Dagwood Bumstead."

During this time the three were approaching an elaborately carved flat-topped desk, where a man was seated, his head bent over a paper on which he was apparently affixing his signature. He added an extra flourish before looking up.

In that brief time, Dagwood and Blondie were busy sizing him up. He appeared to be in his early forties. His thinning, faded brown hair had left a bald spot on the crown of his head. His features were thin and sharp, and his mouth was a narrow, colorless line, in his sallow face. As he raised his head he turned his sharp gray-blue eyes directly at the butler. Quickly, he swept Dagwood with an appraising glance, and then, with a slight start, his gaze fell on Blondie. His mouth settled in a grimmer line, and he looked inquiringly at the butler.

"Mr. and Mrs. Dagwood Bumstead, sir," the butler announced in hollow tones.

As automatically as he would press a button, the man behind the desk turned on a mechanical smile.

"You will pardon my surprise," he said, rising and extending a thin, tapered hand toward Dagwood, "but I was expecting *one* guest."

"Oh, er, uh—my wife thought she'd ride along. Just for the ride, heh, heh," Dagwood babbled in confusion.

"Quite all right, quite all right," the other assured him. "My name is Horace Tyvand." Turning to the butler, he said, crisply, "You will inform Mrs. Tyvand that she has a guest."

"Very good, sir," the butler answered and, with a slight bow, left the room by way of the hallway entrance.

Turning again to Dagwood, the man again flashed a polite smile. "You are 'X-34,' I presume?"

"That's me," Dagwood said. He had regained his composure. "And this is my wife."

"Charmed, I'm sure," Mr. Tyvand answered, with a nod.

"How do you do," Blondie answered stiffly.

"Mrs. Tyvand will be here directly and show you to your room," her host informed Blondie.

It took a moment for Blondie to get over her surprise at that statement. "But I don't need a room! We'll only be here for a short time while you and Dagwood . . . "

"You will be much more comfortable in the ladies' parlor, my dear." His voice had taken on a cutting edge, and his remarks sounded more as though they were orders which he expected to have obeyed.

Dagwood decided to step into the conversation. "If my wife wants to stay here, you haven't any objections, have you?" he demanded.

Swiftly turning to Dagwood, his face knotted in a frown, Tyvand said, sharply. "You, sir—" and then paused, biting his lip. The corners of his lips turned up in another fixed smile as he finished, unctuously.

"Of course I have no objections. I was merely con-
sidering the young lady's comfort." He motioned
them toward a white marble fireplace, flanked with
richly-brocaded Queen Anne sofas. "We might as
well be seated while we carry on our negotiations."

Just then a large, coarse-faced woman, garbed in
a severe black tailored suit, swooped into the room.
She paused to regard Blondie stonily, before
descending on her. She encircled the bewildered
Mrs. Bumstead with a strong arm, apparently bent
on forcefully escorting her out of the room, while
she gushingly said, "You poor dear. You must be
worn to a frazzle. Come upstairs, and you can freshen
up a bit."

In icy tones, which had the effect of making his
wife jerk upright, Tyvand said, "Mrs. Bumstead has
decided to remain here for the time being, Henrietta."

"But I thought—" she began.

Hurriedly, Tyvand cut in, "Henrietta, may I present Mrs Bumstead, and Mr. Bumstead. My wife,
Mrs. Tyvand."

The three murmured acknowledgments. For a
second Mrs. Tyvand studied Blondie's face without
a word, then turned and left the room. Her husband
followed her glance, and found Blondie, puzzled,
looking first at one Tyvand, then at the other.
Blondie stared into space as though searching her

"We Might as Well Be Seated," Tyvand Said

mind for something.

Horace Tyvand watched her, his eyes narrowed. Dagwood fidgeted. He knew Blondie was showing signs of having something on her mind, and he could tell by the way Tyvand regarded her that he was trying to remember something.

Tyvand was the first to speak, and he addressed his words directly at Blondie.

"Mrs. Bumstead, I am afraid the business talk your husband and I are going to have will take longer than you anticipate. Perhaps you would like to return to your home now."

"No, thank you. I won't interfere with your conference," she replied sweetly.

Dagwood smiled. "When Blondie makes up her mind, Mr. Tyvand, you might just as well give up. She has a very strong will. I remember one time—"

"Hush, Dagwood. I think you and Mr. Tyvand should get down to business. The sooner you finish, the sooner we can leave."

"That's right," her husband said, importantly. "How about explaining your proposition, Mr. Tyvand?"

The other man nodded. Then he began his story. First he told how deeply shocked and grieved he and his wife had been to learn that their aunt, Mrs. Billingate, had met a tragic death while they were away.

At this point, Blondie nudged Dagwood, who looked blankly at her.

"I was, of course," continued Tvvand, "over-joyed to learn that there was one person who was intelligent enough, quick-thinking and quick-acting enough, to record the event with a camera. Not one person in a hundred would have been calm and cool at a time like that. and I want to congratulate you, Mr. Bumstead. No doubt you also have a mental photograph of the swittly-moving events."

Dagwood proudly expanded his chest, then felt Blondie's warning tug on his sleeve.

"For that reason, I was anxious to invite you to my home, where I could have the pleasure of meeting you, and consulting you. And I would also like to hear a complete description of the accident as it appeared to you." He paused, then repeated. "As it appeared to you."

"What do you mean appeared—" Dagwood began, but a kick in the shins from Blondie quickly silenced him. Peering at her out of the corner of his eye, he noticed that she had her handkerchief held up in front of her face, as though preparing for a sneeze. He thought she was touching her finger to the space under her nose to stop the sneeze, but her finger was on her lips, silently signaling Dagwood to refrain from talking.

Without knowing why Blondie warned him, but

suspecting that she had a sound reason, Dagwood kept still.

"Were you about to say something?" Tyvand asked.

Dagwood shook his head.

"Hmnn. I thought perhaps you had a comment to make at this point?" Tyvand persisted.

"Uh-uh," Dagwood said, shaking his head more vigorously.

Tyvand squinted his eyes again, his glance darting to Blondie, whose face expressed bland interest, and nothing more.

Tyvand cleared his throat. "As I mentioned, I would like to have the pleasure of consulting you, Mr. Bumstead. I had hoped that you would spend the evening, and perhaps the night, as my guest. Furthermore, I am sure that when you learn how generous I am prepared to be regarding your films, you will feel that, as a gentleman, you can well afford to allow me the pleasure of your company for one night."

They could hear the muffled ring of a telephone from another room.

Tyvand moved quickly toward the door. "You'll pardon me?—the telephone," he said over his shoulder.

The minute he was out of sight, Blondie said, "Look, Dagwood. There's an extension on this desk.

Why didn't he answer it here?"

"Never mind that, Blondie. What I want to know is this—why are you trying to make me keep still? Don't you want me to talk to him? What's the big idea?"

Blondie said, "Don't say a word, Dagwood. He reminds me of a cat playing with a mouse, and you're the mouse."

"*Me?* You're wrong, Blondie. *He's* the mouse. And I've got him purring," Dagwood Bumstead protested.

"Mice don't purr," Blondie said. "But he's purring, and getting ready to pounce. Besides that, Dagwood, there's another angle about him and his horsey-looking wife that I can't quite figure out. But it will come to me, never you mind. The only thing I want to do is to hurry and get out of here. The whole thing gives me the shivers. Did you notice how unfeeling he sounded when he was talking about his aunt?"

"Is that why you poked me a few minutes ago?" Dagwood asked.

"And he's definitely trying to get rid of me," Blondie added.

"Well," Dagwood leaned back on the sofa and thrust his hands in his pockets. "You know how it is with men. When they want to have a good, long talk and a smoke, they don't want any women around." He looked around, anxiously. "I wonder what's taking him so long?"

Blondie said, "I wish I had nerve enough to listen in on that extension line."

"Blondie!" Dagwood was plainly shocked. He held her arm, as though he thought she was going to make a grab for the telephone.

"Don't worry," Blondie laughed. Her gaze wandering around the room, rested on the life-sized portrait above the mantel. It was an oil painting of a girl in her twenties.

Blondie stood up, scrutinizing it with narrowed eyes.

"Oh, I know who that is. It's poor Mrs. Billingate. It must have been painted a long time ago, because on our snapshot she looks a lot older than she does in that picture."

Dagwood took the pictures from his pocket, and picked out the one to which she referred. He held it up toward the portrait, then quickly thrust it back into his pocket, as he saw his host coming through the door.

Blondie said, "She looks to me like a very nice person." Then she noticed Tyvand was returning, and lowered her voice to whisper. "Remember, Dagwood— let *him* do the talking. And don't be such a mouse!"

He couldn't help grinning at her conflicting

orders. "I can't keep quiet as a mouse and act like a cat," he retorted.

"Yes, you can, Dagwood. That's just what I want you to do. You're a cat in disguise. I only hope you can surprise him by pouncing first."

That was too complicated for Dagwood to understand. Before he could tell her so, their host was standing before them, holding out an elegant silver cigarette case. Both Dagwood and Blondie refused politely.

"I smoke a pipe," Dagwood said, then quickly looked at Blondie to see if he had said the wrong thing.

Blondie laughed, and started to tell about the time that Alexander and Alvin had accidently dumped Dagwood's pipe tobacco on the floor, swept it up and poured it back in the humidor, and then wondered why Dagwood turned pale when he started smoking his pipe that night. Before she had finished the story, the telephone in the other room rang again. Hurriedly excusing himself, Tyvand stepped out into the hall.

Puzzled, Blondie and Dagwood looked at each other.

"We're taking up an awful lot of time. And I promised Mrs. Woodley we wouldn't be gone long," Blondie fretted.

"Couldn't we call her from here?" Dagwood suggested. He made a move toward the telephone on the desk, but Mrs. Tyvand made a sudden appearance in the doorway.

"Mr. Tyvand will be back immediately," she told the Bumsteads.

"Would you mind if we used your telephone? I'd like to make an important call," Dagwood asked his hostess.

She seemed genuinely sorry. "I'm afraid you will have to wait a few minutes. Mr. Tyvand is using the line."

Dagwood apologized, "I should have known that. I just didn't think."

Blondie faced Mrs. Tyvand. "As a matter of fact, Mrs. Tyvand, we wondered why he didn't answer his telephone here."

With a deprecatory laugh, Mrs. Tyvand said she was sure it was because he didn't want to bore them with his personal conversation, but she regarded Blondie shrewdly. Then, as abruptly as she had appeared, Mrs. Tyvand left them.

Dagwood shook his head. He couldn't understand Mrs. Tyvand's peculiar behavior.

Then Mr. Tyvand reappeared smilingly from his telephone conversation. He must have received some good news.

Rubbing his hands together, and giving Dagwood no chance to ask about using the telephone, Tyvand said, abruptly, "I am prepared to pay you a thousand dollars for your films and prints."

Dagwood's mouth dropped open.

"Ulp!" was all he could say. Blondie, for some reason of her own, did not seem particularly sur prised or pleased at the announcement. She quietly waited for the man to continue.

Mr. Tyvand continued, "However, I have one stipulation to make. I would like you, also Mrs. Bumstead, to stay here as my guests until tomorrow night, when I will personally put the money into your hands."

"But—but—we—that is, our children," Dagwood began.

"I have a little surprise for you," Tyvand said. "I have included your family in the invitation. What's more, I have taken steps to have them brought over here."

"But—but the puppies—" Dagwood tried again to talk.

"They will be here, too. There is nothing for you to worry about. Relax and enjoy yourselves."

Dagwood turned to Blondie. He couldn't understand her silence.

Tyvand was speaking again. "I will leave you to discuss the invitation," he said, with a sly smile.

Left alone, Dagwood turned to his wife.

"Blondie, it seems too good to be true, but something tells me we shouldn't stay."

Blondie reached for his hand, and held it tightly, saying, in a small, frightened voice, "And something tells me we haven't any choice in the matter."

CHAPTER NINE

THE CAT AND THE MOUSE

Blondie was plainly angry. Dagwood was bewildered, and a feeling of resentment at the high-handed treatment being accorded his family was beginning to show on his frowning face.

"There's something wrong about all this, Blondie. Those pictures aren't worth a thousand dollars to the richest prince in India. Before we do another thing, we're going to try to find out why he's so anxious to get them. What's more, Cookie and Alexander aren't supposed to go out at night. I don't like this." He glowered in the direction of the door.

Abruptly, he went over to it and closed it.

"Blondie, you come here and stand guard. If anyone tries to enter, you slip out and talk to him in the hall. Tell him I'm making a personal phone call, or that I am having a fit—tell him anything, but stall him off for awhile."

"What are you going to do?" Blondie asked.

"I'm going to teach that bird how to play cat and mouse. I'm going to look around and see if I can find out *why* it gives him such tremendous pleasure to have us as his guests."

He hurried over to the desk, and boldly began ex-

amining the papers on top of it. Then he opened the
long, flat drawer nearest the top. Blondie, watching
from the doorway across the room, could see that he
had found a sheaf of papers which apparently caught
his interest.

She snapped her fingers to get his attention, and
told him by sign language that someone was just
outside the door. He nodded, carefully slipped one
of the sheets of paper from the pile, folded it, and
tucked it in his suit-coat pocket. Then he signaled
Blondie to sit on the sofa, and he sat next to her.

When Tyvand, a look of cold fury in his eyes,
stood before them, they were innocently discussing
the style of furniture in the room.

Blondie stood up, and took him completely by
surprise by holding out her hand and exclaiming,
"We have been talking about your invitation, Mr.
Tvvand. We haven't quite decided whether we'll
accept, but we do appreciate being invited."

Her host began rubbing his hands together again,
and his robot-like smile wiped away his furious expression.

"I couldn't take 'no' for an answer," he replied.

Blondie looked inquiringly at Dagwood. He put
his hand up, pretending he was going to wipe his lips
with the back of it, and said in an aside to Blondie,
"Stall."

In a natural voice, he addressed Tyvand.

"What I would like to know is this—is it true that our children are on their way? And if that's true, how did you manage to get them away from the house? I'm sure Mrs. Woodley, the neighbor lady who was staying with them, would not allow them to leave unless she heard from us."

"It was no trouble at all," his host answered. But he offered no further explanation. He changed the subject abruptly, and referred again to the films, reminding Dagwood that he hadn't as yet seen them.

Dagwood laughed jovially.

"As you said, old boy, there's plenty of time. I've never had a thousand dollars worth of pictures before, and it seems kind of nice to hang onto them for awhile."

Mr. Tyvand, although he continued to smile, didn't seem to think Dagwood's remarks were very funny.

He said in a voice that belied the smile, "One would think you didn't trust me. I assure you, I am a man of my word."

"Not at all, not at all," was Dagwood's airy response.

Blondie cut in, with a disarming smile, to say, "One would think *you* didn't trust Dagwood, Mr. Tyvand. I assure you, *he* is a man of *his* word."

There was a brief pause, while Tyvand contemplated the two of them. Dagwood nervously walked to the big double window at the front of the house.

"I wonder where the kids are?" he blurted. "I don't like to have them wandering around in the evening."

"Calm yourself, Bumstead. They'll be here soon enough. I'm sorry about taking them out for the night. I didn't know you disapproved. I merely thought I was providing a treat for all of you," Tyvand said.

"You might have consulted us about it," Dagwood grumbled.

Blondie decided it was about time for her to say something. "Your intentions were good, Mr. Tyvand. Your home is beautiful. How many rooms are there in it?"

"You must go through it, while you are here, Mrs. Bumstead. I'm sure Mrs. Tyvand will be delighted to escort you."

Before she could protest, he had moved quickly toward the door, and pulled a cord. As though awaiting the signal, the butler promptly appeared.

"Inform Mrs. Tyvand that Mrs. Bumstead would like to be shown through the house," Mr. Tyvand said, curtly.

Answering an unspoken appeal from Blondie, Dagwood announced, "Also tell her that Mr. Bumstead wants to see the house, too."

Tyvand shrugged. "It's up to you, Bumstead. Per-

Tyvand Signaled for the Butler

sonally, I would have welcomed an opportunity to have a confidential talk with you."

"Oh, Blondie always listens to my confidential talks," Dagwood blithely informed him. "We can have one later, when we finish our tour."

"That's right," confirmed Blondie. "After awhile, when we have all had a chance to collect our thoughts, we can confide in each other. And maybe we will begin to understand each other better."

Stroking his chin, Tvvand shrewdly studied her. Then he slowly remarked, "There's a possibility we're underestimating each other."

Naively, Blondie retorted, "Oh, I'm sure we're not any brighter than we look."

Before another word could be spoken, Mrs. Tyvand glided into the room, and literally swooped upon the Bumsteads.

"Which room would you like to see first, the game room?" she boomed, as she led them toward the main entrance again.

"Oh, we like games," Dagwood said, but Blondie whispered, "She means the big-game trophy room." So he quickly changed his remark to, "Oh, we like to see the game. Who hunts, your husband?"

"No. The hunting was done many years ago by one of Mrs. Billingate's ancestors. He traveled all over the world," she commented, leading them down a long hallway.

Blondie said to Dagwood, in an undertone, "She's awfully nervous. She isn't doing this because she wants to be a good hostess; she's doing it because that Simon Legree husband of hers ordered her to."

Dagwood whispered back, "She's twice as big as he is."

Blondie smothered a giggle. "She could mop the floor with him if she wanted to—but whatever they have up their sleeves, you can easily see that they're in cahoots on it."

Their hostess turned toward them. "Were you speaking to me?"

"Er—er," Dagwood stuttered.

"Why, yes, Mrs. Tyvand. We were remarking about the size of the building. How many rooms are there?" Blondie said, quickly coming to Dagwood's rescue.

"Eighteen, excluding the servants' quarters," was the reply. She stopped and unlocked a door near the end of the hall. She held the door open, while Dagwood and Blondie entered the room.

"Goodness me," Blondie exclaimed, "Did one man catch them all?"

Mrs. Tyvand seemed annoyed at the question. "Naturally, he was a member of a big expedition," she snapped. Then she continued in a more polite manner, "You will find a plaque under each trophy explaining where and under what circumstances the animal was bagged."

As the room contained at least two dozen mounted heads, including deer, antelope, moose, lions, tigers, leopards, and some specimens the Bumsteads failed to recognize, reading all the plaques appeared to be quite a project. Dagwood was more interested than Blondie in the big display, but Blondie obligingly began to follow him around the room. When she came close to him, he said, barely above a whisper, "Get her to the other end of the room."

Squealing and pointing, Blondie took hold of Mrs. Tyvand's arm, and began pulling her toward the opposite end of the room where a shiny scaled creature gleamed on a small table. With feigned surprise, Blondie said, "Don't tell me you have a stuffed allegozimba!"

"Allegozimba?" Mrs. Tyvand repeated, curiously. "I don't ever remember hearing that name."

"You don't? What is this little animal? I could have sworn it was one of the finest allegozimbas I'd ever had the pleasure to see in a private home."

Mrs. Tyvand laughed apologetically. "I thought it was an anteater. But perhaps you're right."

As she bent to read the plaque, Blondie watched Dagwood out of the corner of her eye. He was on a chair, reaching into the open mouth of a big moosehead. She watched him, while Mrs. Tyvand corrected Blondie concerning the scaly animal. "It's not an allegozimba, I'm afraid, Mrs. Bumstead. This is an aardvark!" she ended triumphantly.

"Imagine my making a mistake like that," Blondie laughed, and also heaved a sigh of relief as she saw that Dagwood had withdrawn his hand from the moose's mouth, climbed down from the chair, and was nonchalantly strolling along to examine another huge head.

Mrs. Tyvand yawned. In the distance, a buzzer sounded. Mrs. Tyvand immediately became alert, and said, "I wonder if you would excuse me for a few minutes? I must speak to one of the servants about preparing your room for the night."

"But, Mrs. Tyvand . . ." Blondie began, protestingly.

"I won't be gone long," the other woman said. She went out, closing the door behind her.

Blondie ran over to Dagwood. "That buzzer was a signal for her to report somewhere," she told him.

"Sh-sh," Dagwood said. "Listen!"

"What are you listening for?" Blondie whispered.

"I wondered whether she would lock the door. But I didn't hear a click."

"We'll soon find out," Blondie said. She ran to the door, tried the knob, then turned to Dagwood. "It's locked."

"Gosh!" Dagwood said, with a sickly smile, as he

looked around the room. "This is a swell den of monstrosities to be cooped in with."

"She'll be back—as soon as she finishes whatever it is that she doesn't want us to know about, Dagwood. Now you tell me what you were fishing for."

"Me? I wasn't fishing. I haven't been fishing since last June, when I caught that big one . . ."

"Never mind that big one. I mean in the moose's mouth. What were you reaching in there for?"

"Oh, that." He looked around cautiously, then leaned close to her to whisper, "I wanted to find out if he liked the taste of film negatives and snapshots."

Blondie's eyes widened, as though she suspected that her husband had suddenly gone berserk. Then she began to understand what he meant.

"You hid them there!" she whispered. "Why?"

"I think that sometime before the evening passes, our genial host expects to get them by hook or by crook. This is a slight precaution in case he tries to get them by crook."

Blondie gazed at him in admiration. "I'm proud of you, Dagwood."

"Thanks, Blondie. But that doesn't get us out of this room. And it doesn't tell us where to find our children."

"Do you suppose he's just bluffing?" she asked, hopefully.

Dagwood shook his head. "I don't think he's bluffing about that. And if I know our little family, we'll certainly know it when they arrive."

After trying in vain again to open the door, Blondie sat on one of the ugly, massive chairs and cupped her chin in her hand. She closed her eyes, lost in thought. Suddenly she asked, "Dagwood, what did you find in the desk?"

He lowered his voice to answer. "We've got to make sure there is no one watching or listening," he said. "I want to show you something."

Quickly moving to the door, he stooped to peep through the keyhole, then went to each of the two side windows. It was growing dark outside, as Blondie joined her husband at the windows.

"We could jump it from here, if they think they have us locked in," Dagwood commented. Then he jerked to attention.

"Look, Blondie. There's that woman in the green coat! The one that ran into me that day! She's going into the garage. What do you know about that? What do you suppose she's doing here? Things begin to look more and more suspicious. Let's break a window and make a dash for home!"

"But we can't, Dagwood. If what Mr. Tyvand says is true, and he really *has* sent for the children, we can't leave them here!"

"That's right. Besides, there's a high wall around the property, and you can be sure the gate isn't unlocked."

"Oh, dear," Blondie said, plaintively, "I wish we knew what will happen next. Dagwood, what about that paper?"

"Oh, yes, see what you can make out of it, Blondie. There were several of the same type, with different initials at the top. I took this one off the bottom, thinking it wouldn't be missed as quickly as the others might."

Blondie studied the typewritten sheet. It was written on the same high-quality paper, and with the same light slanting script as the unsigned letter that Dagwood had received in answer to his advertisement.

At the top of the sheet was the notation, in ink, "Instructions for S. R." That was as far as Blondie got, for hearing a slight sound at the door, Dagwood snatched the paper from her, and quickly thrust it in an inner pocket.

Rushing to the door, Dagwood and Blondie waited expectantly for it to open. Nothing happened, and Dagwood rattled the knob.

"It sounded to me like scratching," Blondie said.

She and her husband both got the same idea at the exact moment. They crouched down on all fours, and tried to look under the small space beneath the door.

They could see four small, white paws.

"See What You Can Make of It," Dagwood Said

"Elmer," Dagwood whispered. He heard an answering whine from the puppy. Footsteps along the
hallway could also be heard. The Bumsteads stood
up, brushed themselves off, and waited for the door
to open. They waited in vain. Then they crouched
down again. The four white paws were no longer
there.

Angrily, Dagwood declared, "I've had about
enough of this!" He grabbed the doorknob as
though determined to shake it loose, when, to his
amazement and consternation, the door flew open.

Hands in pockets, and rocking on his heels, Horace Tyvand confronted them, pleasantly inquiring,
"Well, did you enjoy the game room?"

"Enjoy it!" Dagwood exploded. "What was the
big idea of having us locked inside?"

His tones indicating shock and hurt feelings, Tyvand said, "You amaze me, Mr. Bumstead. You
weren't locked in—you must have imagined it."

Blondie said, "Then I must have imagined it, too,
Mr. Tyvand. I tried the door and couldn't get it
open, either!"

"That's strange." He rattled and turned the knob
from both sides of the door. "Perhaps it caught.
This is a century-old building, you know, and some
of its fixtures are beginning to show their age."

Dagwood thrust out his chin, but before he could
say a word, a queer little sound from Blondie halted

him.

"Prrr, prrrr," she said, but it was enough to remind him that his host was again enacting a cat-and mouse scene.

"Did you say something, Mrs. Bumstead?" Tyvand asked.

"Not a word," Blondie replied, honestly. "But we have seen only one room. Your wife promised to show us some more, but she was unexpectedly called away."

"She'll be back shortly," Blondie was assured. "There she is now."

Mrs. Tyvand was swiftly coming toward them. She panted, breathlessly inquiring, "Have I kept you waiting long? I'm frightfully sorry."

Blondie nudged Dagwood, slyly calling his attention to tiny scratches on Mrs. Tyvand's arm. Her lips formed the word "El-mer," but she didn't speak the name. Dagwood bowed his head to let her know that he understood.

"Can we see the children now?" Blondie asked pleasantly.

Taken aback, Tyvand paused before blandly replying, "They have not arrived as yet, Mrs. Bumstead. You can rest assured that we will inform you the moment they get here."

With a warning frown, Blondie again stopped Dagwood from speaking. Her look said, "Proceed with caution."

Blondie said, "Perhaps you wouldn't mind if I used your telephone? I would like to call home to see if they are still there."

Horace and Henrietta Tyvand exchanged quick glances.

"I'll be glad to put in the call for you, Mrs. Bumstead," Mrs. Tyvand said. "Would you tell me your number?"

"Why, yes," Blondie replied in a grateful manner. "The number is Adams 2-3-0."

Dagwood had heard that number before, but he knew it was not his telephone number. It was a number he had used quite recently, too, he felt sure. Then he remembered what it was. It was the police station.

Quizzically, he glanced at Blondie, wondering what good it would do them to have Mrs. Tyvand get the police station by mistake. But her reassuring smile conveyed the message that she had a good reason percolating in her pretty head.

Mrs. Tyvand picked up the hall telephone, called the number, and then asked, "Is this the Dagwood Bumstead residence?"

She turned from the instrument with a scowl, clicked down the receiver, waited a moment, then tried again. Again she asked, "Is this the Dagwood Bumstead residence?"

The telephone almost jumped out of her hand at the explosive verbal battery of words that squawked over the line. Mrs. Tyvand quietly replaced the receiver, remarking, "Perhaps it would be better to wait and try again later."

The Bumsteads, reluctant but trying to appear willing, continued their tour of the old manor under the watchful eye of the hostess. Her husband withdrew, following a murmured apology. During their walk, they managed to have a few whispered words together.

Dagwood questioned her about giving the police telephone number.

"I knew there was no one at our house. And the only thing I could think of to do was to have her call the police. That was the only number I could think of, off-hand."

"Are you sure that was the only reason?"

"Well-ll," Blondie admitted, "I was hoping that they might be annoyed enough to pay attention to the call."

"That's a good idea, Blondie," Dagwood said. "The more anyone can annoy that sergeant at the desk, the better I like it."

"That isn't what I meant, Dagwood. But never mind. It probably won't work out right anyway," she sighed.

They had gone into the fifth room. The walls

were lined with family portraits. Aloud they admired them and murmured polite praise of the art
work.

Suddenly, Blondie jerked Dagwood's sleeve.
"That one right across from here, Dagwood. Did
you ever see such a murderous-looking individual
as that?"

She had spoken in an undertone, but their hostess
apparently was paying attention. Their reference to
the portrait was obviously highly distasteful to her,
for she drew back, her nostrils quivering, and stonily invited them to go to a corner of the room to see
a childhood crayon portrait of the late Mrs. Billingate. She stalked away, expecting to be immediately
followed, which gave Dagwood and Blondie another
opportunity for hurried conversation.

Dagwood said, "Does he remind you of the same
person he reminds me of?"

Blondie nodded. "Except for the hat, and the
fiendish expression, he looks somewhat like Horace Tvvand."

Her husband agreed, and continued to study the
portrait. "It almost seems as though I've seen this
picture before."

Blondie continued to gaze at it, too. Then she
clutched Dagwood's arm.

"We've seen a duplicate of it—right in our own
house, Dagwood. The hat, the expression, and all.

We looked at it in our very own basement. Think hard, Dagwood. I'm only guessing, and if *you* get the same idea. . . ."

In a tense whisper, Dagwood said, "On Cookie's picture! Blondie, that's Horace Tyvand in the background of that picture. Have we got that one with us, so we can make sure?"

"No, thank goodness. That one's home," Blondie whispered back.

"What do you mean 'thank goodness?' " Dagwood asked.

"That's our ace in the hole, Dagwood," was all Blondie had time to whisper, just before Mrs. Tyvand's frowning face turned toward her. She quickly ran to her hostess' side, and feigned interest in the childhood crayon portrait of the late Mrs. Billingate.

Before they again joined their host in the drawing room, Blondie had time to utter one more admonition. "Pretend you're falling in with all of their plans," she whispered.

Dagwood remembered to ask Mrs. Tyvand to put in another call for their home, explaining that he and Blondie were naturally quite concerned over the delay in the arrival of their family. With apparent reluctance, she tried again to call the Bumstead residence, and was annoyed to find that she again had the wrong number.

"The same man seems to be answering every

time," she commented, but when Blondie offered to attempt to put the call through, her request was politely, but tactfully, refused.

"Shall we rest awhile, before going upstairs?" Mrs. Tyvand suggested. Without waiting for a reply, she indicated that Dagwood and Blondie were again to sit on the sofa beside the fireplace.

The Tyvands sat opposite them. "Have you decided to stay for the night?" Mr. Tyvand inquired. He looked at Dagwood, but Blondie answered the question.

"We feel rather out of place in such a gorgeous mansion, Mr. Tyvand, but I think it will be fun for us to pretend we live here, just for one night." She smiled sweetly at their host.

It was difficult to determine which of the three listeners was the more amazed at her statement. Dagwood's mouth dropped open. Tyvand smiled mechanically, and began to rub his hands together, a pleased expression quickly covering his incredulity. Mrs. Tyvand looked inquiringly at Blondie, and then at her husband.

"Fine, fine," Tyvand said, a crafty look coming over his face.

Dagwood chimed in with the lead Blondie had given him. "We aren't used to having invitations for our whole family showered on us," he said, with a short laugh. "The children must have the right kind of food, and plenty of milk. And the puppies. . . ."

Chidingly, Blondie stopped him. "We don't want to bother the Tyvands with all the details of their diet, Dagwood. I can fix their breakfast myself in the morning, if Mrs. Tyvand will permit it?" She smiled sweetly, and was assured that this arrangement would be possible.

Tyvand addressed Dagwood, "While we are relaxed and comfortable, shall we glance over those pictures, Bumstead?"

Obligingly, Dagwood reached into his pocket. He frowned, reached in another pocket, then hurriedly searched through all of them. He whistled, stood up, and quickly dug into all of his pockets again.

"What's the matter?" Tyvand demanded.

"Did you forget them?" Blondie asked in an anxious tone

"Are they lost?" Mrs. Tyvand snapped.

"Gosh, that's funny," Dagwood said. "I had them with me when I came here."

He observed that the Tyvands were looking at each other. Both shook their heads negatively. Tyvand walked to the door, and tugged the bell cord to summon the butler. Blondie bit her lip to suppress a smile, as her host grilled his servant about the pictures. He was not only amazed but resentful at being accused of having a knowledge of the missing films.

Tyvand turned abruptly to Dagwood, who said, smoothly, "I think I might have jerked them out of my pocket when I reached for my hankie while we were going through the rooms. Shall we organize a hunting party?"

There was another quick exchange of glances between the Tyvands, and this time the butler was included. Again rubbing his hands together, Horace Tyvand raised a polite objection.

"If they are there, we can find them later," he said. "In the meantime, would you like to go to your room to freshen up a bit?"

"Oh, yes," Blondie said, hurriedly, nudging Dagwood's elbow.

"Oh, yes," Dagwood echoed. "But I would like to check up on the family."

Tyvand turned to Blondie. "Why don't you make the call from this telephone?" he said, indicating the one on the desk.

"Thank you," Blondie replied. Hurriedly, she called Adams 2-3-0. After asking if she was connected with the Dagwood Bumstead residence, there seemed to be a long pause. The Tyvands were observing her with suspicion, and Dagwood began to get restless. What was she waiting for?

Then she said, into the telephone, "Why, Pete Howard! Excuse me. I've tried *three* or *four* times to call the Bumsteads, and who do I always get but you?"

Tyvand snatched the telephone from her. "Are you sure you gave the operator the correct number?" he snarled. Dagwood jumped to his feet, his fists clenched, but Blondie had the situation in hand. She patted Mr. Tyvand on the cheek.

"My, but you are a frightening man," she said, timidly.

Tyvand regained his composure, replaced the telephone, and changed his tone of voice.

Running his fingers under his collar and straightening his tie, he apologized. "It makes me angry to have poor telephone service, especially when I have guests."

Blondie smiled forgiveness, and beckoned to Dagwood.

"Shall we go to our room, dear?" she asked.

They were escorted by the haughty butler to a room on the second floor. After bowing them into their room, he made a dignified retreat.

Both Dagwood and Blondie waited a moment then made a dash toward the door. To their relief, the knob turned, and with a slight tug, it opened a few inches. Dagwood peeped through the opening, then threw the door open wide.

"Look, Blondie! There's Elmer!"

The puppy looked up happily, holding something black in his mouth.

"What's that?" Dagwood asked.

Quickly, Blondie stooped and coaxed Elmer into releasing his prize. She held it up and cried out happily:

"Dagwood, Elmer found the tramp's whiskers!"

CHAPTER TEN

SOLVING THE PUZZLE

Elmer found himself whisked into the room with his amazed master and mistress. He jumped up in the air, trying to retrieve the false beard, but Blondie tightened her grasp on it, and petted Elmer to keep him quiet.

"We've got to work fast, Dagwood. Those people shoved us up here so they could tear around downstairs looking for those films, which you cleverly hid."

"I know," Dagwood acknowledged, proudly. "I knew I had to think up some way for us to be alone so we could talk this thing over and decide what we want to do. Do you think Elmer can lead us to the children?"

"I'm not worried about the children, Dagwood. They'll be well treated, at least until the Tyvands decide not to be polite. I'm hoping Elmer will lead us to the place where he found these whiskers, and perhaps we can find some more parts to fit into this puzzle. But we can't waste any time!" She knelt beside the puppy, and showed him the false whiskers. "Put them back where you got them, Elmer," she said, sternly.

Elmer stopped wagging his tail, and with an air of deep dejection, took the whiskers from her and stood by the door, waiting for Blondie to open it.

"We'll follow him," Blondie instructed.

The puppy started down the hall, turning to see if Blondie and Dagwood were following. Satisfied that they were behind him, he kept going.

"He seems to be leading us back to the servants' quarters," Blondie said. They stopped and waited while Elmer dropped the beard, and took his time about picking it up again.

"Take it back where you found it, Elmer," Blondie said, as loudly as she dared.

Elmer stopped at a door slightly ajar, at the end of the hall. Dagwood opened it, and found that it led to another hallway, two steps down and narrower than the one they were leaving. Passing two more doorways, Elmer finally came to a halt before a third. He dropped the false whiskers in front of it. Then he looked up at Blondie, and began wagging his tail happily, as if awaiting praise for obeying orders.

Blondie patted him.

"Don't let him get away," Dagwood whispered. "He can probably lead us to the children as soon as we find out what's in here."

"Maybe they're in there," Blondie said, hopefully, as Dagwood opened the door. Blondie picked up Elmer and held him in her arms. He snuggled down

Blondie Held Elmer in Her Arms

comfortably.

"They aren't in here," Dagwood said in disappointment. "This is just a clothes closet." He reached inside and pulled a light cord. A dim bulb on the sidewall shed light on an odd assortment of clothes. Some were on hangers, and others were on hooks.

"Look, Dagwood!" Blondie exclaimed, pointing to a plaid shawl. "That looks just like Mrs. Wiskulouski's shawl, doesn't it?"

"Maybe it *is* her shawl," Dagwood whispered. "Let's see if there are any other interesting items here."

He pawed over the clothes.

"Here's a pin-stripe suit. Remember that day of the accident—I told you when I went back there a man in a pin-stripe suit bawled me out? This looks like his suit."

"Maybe it is his suit," Blondie said, absently reiterating Dagwood's statement about the shawl.

"And here are the tramp clothes to go with the beard! I think we make wonderful detectives, Blondie. Only I wish I knew what we were trying to detect. Have you any ideas, Blondie?"

"I'm beginning to have some. I think we have all the different parts to our problem. Now we have to calmly arrange them in order so we get the right answer when we put them all together."

Elmer began to whimper, immediately demanding their attention.

"I think the best thing to do now, Dagwood, is to release Elmer, find out if the children are all right, and then sneak back to our room before the Tyvands discover that we've been snooping."

"Okay," Dagwood agreed. He whispered to Elmer, "Find Alexander."

"Erf!" Elmer barked, and wriggled out of Blondie's arms to scuttle down the hallway. They tiptoed after him, and soon came to a stairway. After descending to the first landing, Elmer stopped, looking triumphantly at his master and mistress.

His finger at his lips to caution silence, Dagwood quietly turned the knob of the door on the landing and opened it a crack.

A woman's voice was saying, "But I've read that story to you six times now! What's the matter with you, kid! Don'tcha know how to play?"

Alexander's voice replied, "But Cookie. Daisy, and the puppies like to hear the story, too. We like the way your nose wiggles when you talk."

"For the luva mike!" the woman exclaimed.

Blondie whispered, excitedly, "That's Mrs. Wiskulouski, and she's talking English!"

"Sh-sh," Dagwood cautioned. They listened again.

"If you stop reading, Cookie will cry, Daisy will

bark, and the puppies will squeak. You said you were going to take us to see mother and father. Why don't you take us there?" Alexander said.

Blondie whispered, "He shouldn't be saucy to a grown person."

Dagwood grinned. "He's doing all right." The woman hastily began to read again the story of Sukey the Simple Wearing Her Wimple.

Leaving the door slightly ajar to enable Elmer to paw his way back into the room, Blondie and Dagwood quietly but hastily returned to the room which had been assigned to them by the Tyvands.

"It should take that trio downstairs quite a while to search for the pictures. That gives us a chance to try to fit our clues together," Dagwood said. "But first, Blondie, tell me about that funny telephone call you made downstairs. Did you really talk to Pete Howard?"

Blondie smiled as she shook her head in the negative. "I was trying to be clever, but I don't think it will work. The desk sergeant told me he was getting sick and tired of having people ask him if the Dagwood Bumstead residence was there. I waited until he had finished ranting, then I tapped three times, paused, and tapped four times. Then I said, 'Pete Howard, ex-cuse me,' and mentioned I'd tried *three* or *four* times. Get it, Dagwood? If Pete Howard should happen to come into the station, which he should sometime between now and the time he meets his deadline tomorrow, there's a slight chance they'll tell him about it."

"What good would that do us?"

"He might start to think about it. X-34 was the number of your blind ad. He might be able to find out who put it in the paper by mentioning that there's something funny and mysterious about you. That should start him to thinking."

"He still wouldn't know where we were or how to help us, would he?" dubiously inquired Dagwood. "It was a bright idea, Blondie, but far-fetched."

"Maybe another one will come to me," Blondie said. "Now, let me see that paper you smuggled out of Tyvand's desk."

This time, Blondie was able to read it through without interruption. Under the notation in hand-writing, "Instructions for S. R.," Blondie read the following typewritten paragraphs:

"Remember, if you are questioned about having seen anyone else in the crowd, and are told to describe them, first mention one or two other people before you sandwich in descriptions of Joe and Maggie.

"Be sure to tell about Joe's suit being striped. Mention Maggie's shawl. When you make up descriptions of other people, whatever you do, don't mention anyone that might be taken for Bumstead. If they try to pin you down about him, just look blank and say you don't remember seeing anyone there answering to that description.

"Don't mention the child in the carriage, unless the examiner mentions it first, or you will find yourself trapped.

"This Dagwood Bumstead, or any members of his family, will not appear at the inquest. You can trust me to attend to that. He's a saphead that can be easily handled without using rough tactics, although if necessary they may be used.

"Without his films and snapshots, his testimony won't hold water against three witnesses whose stories all fit together. The police swallowed them, and the coroner thinks you are doing him a favor in testifying.

"You will receive your share of the money when the will is probated shortly after the inquest. Report back to the manor when you finish your testimony."

Plainly shocked at the implications of what she read, Blondie paused and stared into space. Things were rapidly beginning to take shape, she told her husband. He was beginning to get a glimmering of what it was all about, too.

"Remember, Blondie, I told you that the witnesses who talked to the police didn't see what I saw."

Blondie nodded. "And for a very good reason, Dagwood. They were *told* what to say they saw. They never mentioned the other car."

"And Horace Tyvand was driving the other car! He was supposed to be out of town. We've got—" he hesitated, glancing around the room cautiously. Blondie held her finger to her lips. She leaned close, and whispered into his ear, "Don't even mention our ace in the hole, dear."

"Do you think someone might be listening?"

"We can't be sure," Blondie whispered.

"I've got an idea. Let's make out a report."

"Oh, Dagwood! You and your reports! We haven't any paper."

"A good host would provide some. Let's look around."

There was a small desk in the corner which yielded some stationery initialed "B."

Dagwood snickered. "I have to laugh when I think how smug he was telling about the films And now he's chasing around like mad downstairs looking for them. So I'm a saphead, am I! Wait until he finds out that *he's* the sap.".

"We'll have to be careful, Dagwood. He hinted that there might be rough stuff if you weren't the saphead he thought you."

Thoughtfully, Dagwood chewed his pencil.

"We've got to be careful. And we'll have to get out of here. But as long as the children are here, we can't and won't leave, and Tyvand is smart enough to know that. We'll try to outsmart him, that's what we'll do," he concluded.

Blondie shook her head sorrowfully as she gazed at Dagwood. "What have we been trying to do all this time, dear?"

"That's right. We've been outsmarting him. But we must keep right on outsmarting him," Dagwood declared. Blondie nodded.

"We'll both write the report," Blondie suggested. "First I'll write what I think, and then you write what you think."

Dagwood agreed and leaned over Blondie's shoulder as she wrote:

"Mr. and Mrs. Horace Tyvand were supposed to be out of town at the time of the accident. They were not out of town. They were right there, at the corner of Third and Grand, at the time it happened. A car crowded Mrs. Billingate's car into the lamppost—"

Dagwood snatched the pencil from her hand, and excitedly added, "Horace Tyvand was driving the car that crowded Mrs. Billingate's car."

He gave Blondie the pencil again.

*Dagwood Leaned Over Blondie's Shoulder as
She Wrote*

"An innocent bystander, name of Dagwood Bumstead, happened to be there at the same time and
took some pictures.

"A woman in a green coat, later seen at the
manor, almost knocked the camera to the ground,
but luckily Dagwood's son caught it.

"Mr. Bumstead returned later to find out more
about it, when a man in a pin-stripe suit scared him
away."

Dagwood grabbed the pencil again to protest, in
writing, "I wasn't scared."

Blondie crossed out that line, and wrote, "A
tramp invaded the Bumstead home. Evidence showed he was looking for something. Mr. Bumstead was
attacked, and strands from a false beard were
found."

Again Dagwood took the pencil from her. "Butler looked familiar. Possibility he was not only man
in pin-stripe suit, but disguised as tramp later."

Blondie looked at him in surprise. That was an
angle she hadn't thought about.

He continued to write, "Mrs. Billingate's car was
crowded into post, but jolt might not have proved
fatal. How did she happen to be there?"

Blondie pondered the question for a few minutes, and then she wrote, hurriedly, "Newspaper
article said she seldom drove car. Must have received
orders, or alarming news, to make her go out alone.

Whoever sent for her must have given directions, to be sure she'd pass a certain corner."

Again it was Dagwood's turn to write. He thought hard. Then he began to write fast.

"Witnesses' were stationed at the corner. I mean *planted* at the corner. Three of them, the butler, the woman in the green coat, and Mrs. W. (I don't know how to spell it.)"

Blondie suddenly remembered something. She added, "*News* item said victim died of shock."

She looked at Dagwood. Horror filled her eyes as she resumed writing, slowly forming the ominous words, "Someone who knew she shouldn't be shocked provided the shock. Why?"

Aghast at the startling trend their deductions were following, Dagwood walked back and forth, deeply worried, before writing, "Horace Tyvand was only living relative and sole heir of the Billingate estate."

He began pacing the floor again. Blondie wrung her hands in perplexity and fear.

She walked to the front window and stared outside. Dagwood came over to her, and put a protective arm about her.

"We'll get out of this somehow, Blondie," he said. "Don't worry."

"If only the children weren't here, Dagwood. We've got to get away!"

Dagwood cupped her chin in his hands, and looked into her eyes. "That isn't all we must do, Blondie. We've got to do something, anything, to keep these fiends from going through with their plot."

Blondie's eyes filled with tears. "When I think of that poor Mrs. Billingate, trusting them, and then having them—" she couldn't finish.

Dagwood patted her, comfortingly. "And here's us, right in the middle of the whole thing."

Blondie's shoulders straightened. "But we're not helpless, Dagwood."

"And we're not afraid," Dagwood said.

"Of course not. We'll figure something out. If we could only get the children safely out of here!"

They stood there. absorbed in their thoughts. trying to figure out what they should do next. They had their backs to the room, and failed to notice that the door had been opened. Horace Tyvand entered the room. He narrowed his eyes, regarding them in silence. then his glance rested on the papers on which Dagwood and Blondie had been writing at the desk. Still unobserved by the Bumsteads, he picked them up and began to read them.

One of the sheets of the stationery rattled as he turned it over. Startled at the sound, Blondie turned and smothered a scream.

Quickly, Dagwood turned to see what had frightened her. He clenched his fists and bit his lip, breathing heavily, as he watched to see what Horace Tyvand's next move would be.

For what seemed an interminable length of time to Dagwood and Blondie, Tyvand silently read the penciled notes. Blondie's hand found Dagwood's, and they stood there like two culprits awaiting sentence. Dagwood squeezed Blondie's hand in what he hoped was a reassuring manner, but his knees shook and he had to struggle to keep his teeth from chattering.

A commotion from another part of the house broke the silence, but none of the three moved. The Bumsteads, as though turned into stone images, faced Horace Tyvand. As he finished the last page of notes, he pursed his lips, and then bestowed on the pair his mirthless smile.

For a moment he did not speak but stood there, apparently to enjoy having them at his mercy.

"It seems," he said, contemptuously, "that I have made the mistake of underestimating you."

"Prrr, prrrr," Blondie answered, for Dagwood's benefit.

That tiny sound served to jerk Dagwood back to normal. He forgot his terror and tried to muster a laugh.

"Ha! We've been trying to figure out why you were willing to pay a thousand dollars for my films," he said.

Blondie tittered. "A thousand dollars looks like a million to us. But if you want to part with your money, that's your business."

Dagwood had an inspiration. He pointed to the papers in Tyvand's hands, and lied glibly, "We made out that report to give you to let you know that we know how valuable our films and pictures are to you. We knew you were a shrewd business-man, Mr. Tyvand. We didn't underestimate *you*. We got tired of having you act as if you were being so nice to us for the pure joy of it."

Blondie held her breath. Dagwood was playing a long chance, trying to convince Tyvand that all cards were being laid on the table in full view.

Would Tyvand swallow the bait?

A crafty expression crossed his face, and he smiled again. This time there was a glimmer of real amuse-ment in his eyes. He was obviously laughing to him-self at the expense of the Bumsteads.

The sound of a commotion down the hall grew louder, until it amounted to a full-sized clamor out-side the door of the room where the Bumsteads and Tyvand were talking.

Flinging the door open wide, a disheveled woman, known to Blondie as Mrs. Wiskulouski, stood defi-antly facing them. She was completely surrounded by members of the Bumstead family. She held Cookie, who playfully tugged at her hair. With the

other hand she held tightly to Alexander. Daisy and
two of her five puppies were jumping up at the
woman, who had a difficult time maintaining her
balance.

"I've had plenty of this outfit," she shouted.
"Take this—this *zoo* off my hands. I still gotta chase
two of the mutts—"

"Three," Blondie corrected.

The woman glowered at her. "Three, then. *She*,"
she said, indicating with her head the general direction of the downstairs, "told me to give 'em exercise.
Give *them* exercise! I ain't never had so much exercise myself since . . ."

"Calm yourself, Maggie," Tyvand interrupted.

Dagwood cut in, "I thought you said the children
were not here."

"Here! They're here. I'll say," said Maggie, bel-
ligerently. "And you sure can have 'em."

She thrust Cookie toward Blondie, who hugged
the little girl in a warm embrace. Alexander ran to
her, and she lovingly ran her fingers through his unruly hair. Daisy yelped joyfully, and the two puppies raced around the room.

Maggie thrust out her chin at Tyvand. "Hang on
to these while I round up the others."

"Maggie!" he said, angrily. But Maggie had lung-
ed down the hall at full speed. Tyvand took two
steps forward, apparently bent on following her,

then changed his mind. He addressed Blondie, "I was about to notify you that your family had arrived, Mrs. Bumstead. That was the reason I came up here."

"Thank you," Blondie said, forcing a smile.

"Did you find what you were looking for?" Dagwood asked.

Tyvand seemed mildly surprised at the question. "What I was looking for? I wasn't looking for anything, Bumstead."

"I thought perhaps you . . ." Dagwood began. But he found Cookie thrust into his arms by Blondie, who said, in an undertone, "Shush!"

"You thought *what?*" Tyvand urged.

"Oh, er, the puppies. Were you looking for the puppies?"

"No. I was *not* looking for the puppies. I was not looking for anything. I merely wanted you and your wife to have a few moments to rest and freshen up." His voice was raised almost to a shout to make himself heard above the hubbub in the room. He lost his air of suave politeness. "Confound it! Can't you shut those brats up?"

"Look here, Tyvand," Dagwood yelled. "You are referring to members of my family!"

"Well, keep the members of your family quiet!" Tyvand shouted back at him.

"If they don't want to be quiet they don't have to

"Your Family Has Arrived," Tyvand Announced

be! You don't understand children . . ." Dagwood
continued at the top of his voice, as he waved his
one free hand.

"I'll talk to you later!" Tyvand ground out between clenched teeth.

"I don't care if I never talk to you again!" was
Dagwood's angry retort.

Blondie, with a quiet admonition, silenced the
two children and Daisy. The two pups, apparently
tiring of frolicking around, pantingly stopped to
rest.

"Aren't we losing control of ourselves?" she inquired in a natural tone.

The two men, glaring at each other, said nothing.
Tyvand was the first to regain his composure.

"We obviously can't talk while this pandemonium
is about to break loose," Tyvand said. "After the
others are brought in, and they all settle down for
the night, you can come downstairs and we'll resume our conversation."

He gave them no alternative, but stalked out of
the room, closing the door after him.

Blondie hastily instructed Dagwood to leave, too.
"Offer to help round up the pups, Dagwood.
They're probably running around outdoors, and
you can tell him they'll come when you call. While
you are out there, look around and see if there is
any way to escape from this place except through the

front gate."

She took Cookie from him, and put the child on the bed.

"Tell that Maggie to heat some milk for Cookie, and to bring a glass of milk and some graham crackers for Alexander. Also, tell her to fix a big bowl of bread cubes and milk for the puppies. If you can't find her, ask Mrs. Tyvand. Tell her that otherwise none of them will go to sleep, and none of the rest of us will get any peace."

"But, Blondie, I think we should tell him we want to go home right now. I'll tell him I know where the films and pictures disappeared, and offer to help find them," Dagwood protested.

"You're forgetting, Dagwood, that we have a mission to perform. We are the only people who can do anything to spoil all their plans."

"But the children?"

"Where can they be safer than with us?" Blondie countered.

Without further argument, Dagwood, with trepidation, went to the door. He was afraid to try to open it for fear it would be locked. Greatly relieved, he discovered that the knob turned and he lost no time in running after his host.

It took a lot of persuasive talk, but Dagwood, trying to hide his intense dislike of the man, convinced Tyvand that the only way they would be able to get

the runaway dogs settled for the night was to have
him, Dagwood, go outdoors after them.

Tyvand stroked his chin. "You wouldn't by any
chance be thinking of abandoning my hospitality,
would you? Because if you are, you might as well
give up that idea. As long as you are being perfectly
frank with me," he indicated the penciled sheets in
his hand, "I am willing to be perfectly frank with
you. You would be wasting your time looking for a
way out without my permission. Furthermore, you
have a wife and family upstairs who might not enjoy being left here without your protecting wing
shielding them."

There was a veiled threat in his words, which
Dagwood pretended to ignore.

"I'm just beginning to enjoy myself here, Mr.
Tyvand," Dagwood said, with what he hoped sounded like disarming frankness. "And I hope we can
return the invitation by inviting you and your wife
to visit us sometime."

Tyvand stroked his chin again, regarding Dagwood in a manner which indicated that Dagwood
was one of the most peculiar specimens he had ever
encountered.

Taking advantage of the momentary weakening
in Tyvand's attitude, Dagwood hastily rattled off
Blondie's orders about the milk and food for the
children and the dogs.

"Very well," Tyvand snapped, glancing at his watch. "It shouldn't take more than ten minutes for you to return with those mongrels."

A protest against calling the dogs mongrels rose to Dagwood's lips but he held back, satisfied that Tyvand was about to unbolt and unlock the front door.

Dagwood drew in a deep breath of fresh air when he got outside. Then he remembered, with only ten minutes allotted him, he had a lot of territory to cover.

He knew he could summon the dog, Elmer, by whistling, and Elmer's sister-pups would follow. He could do that at the last minute. He also knew from observation when they arrived in the afternoon that there were no openings, besides the big front gate, along the front wall around the estate. He headed to the side and stumbled along in the darkness until he felt the cold stone of the wall. Carefully feeling his way along, he went the full length of it to a corner, which he assumed to be the rear boundary of the property.

He covered about half a block along the back wall, and then came to the iron bars of a huge gate. He rattled and shook it with all his might, but it was securely fastened. He knelt to feel how high it was from the ground. He heard a low whine, and then felt a moist wet tongue licking his hand.

"Elmer!" he chuckled, patting the dog. "Where'd you come from, the other side of the gate?" Elmer was joined by the other missing puppies, who climbed all over Dagwood in wild ecstasy. Dagwood satisfied himself that the gate was high enough from the ground for a small puppy to scramble under, but no higher.

He heard a woman's voice calling, "Here, dogs!" With a smile, he gathered the three puppies in his arms and started back to the manor.

Instead of going directly in the back way, where the kitchen lights blazed, Dagwood circled the huge structure, studying the outside of the building. He located the room where he and his family were to spend the night, but in the darkness it was impossible to figure out whether it was possible to climb down the two stories from any of the windows.

Still carrying the puppies, he went up the front porch steps. The front door was open, and Tyvand was standing there, Mrs. Tyvand at his side. They appeared to be quarreling, but at sight of Dagwood, they stopped talking.

"I found them!" Dagwood announced.

Mrs. Tyvand said, "Don't set them down. Take them right up to your room!"

Her husband used a more polite tone. "We should be pleased to have you join us in the drawing room after your family has retired for the night. Maggie and Tompkins will fix cots in your room."

"How about the food?" Dagwood asked.

Mrs. Tyvand answered, "That has been sent up."

"Fine," Dagwood said, beginning to mount the steps. "We'll see you later."

They had no trouble getting Cookie to sleep. She was tired from all of the unusual excitement, but this same excitement had exactly the opposite effect on Alexander. Daisy and her pups curled up on a big, soft rug.

"Are we always going to be rich like this?" Alexander wanted to know.

"No, dear," Blondie said. "We are going back to our cozy little home tomorrow. Go to sleep and dream about it."

"But I like being rich, Mama," Alexander insisted. "Then I can tell Alvin all about it. Maybe we could get some polo ponies."

Dagwood laughed. "We wouldn't be able to eat if we had polo ponies, Alexander. The pups almost eat us out of house and home, now."

"Just the same," Alexander murmured drowsily, "I would climb up on one of them, ride past Alvin's house, and . . ." He was asleep before he had finished talking.

Blondie laughed, and whispered, "He can ride the polo ponies in his dreams."

"As far as I'm concerned," Dagwood said, "that's as close as he'll ever come to it. By the way, Blondie, Tyvand and his wife were arguing about something, but they stopped when I came in with the puppies."

"Then they must have been fighting about us, Dagwood. I wouldn't be surprised but that he's willing to trust us, thinking that we will keep quiet because we want the thousand dollars. But he still hasn't got the films and pictures. She apparently doesn't want him to let us go. She is probably trying to make him keep us here until after the inquest tomorrow."

Dagwood thought this over, and had an idea.

"Let's talk about the money again, then, Blondie. And we can offer to find the pictures and films. I can hint that I know where they are. If he lets us leave the first thing in the morning, we can spoil his plans from the outside better than we can from the inside."

"I think you're right, Dagwood," Blondie acknowledged. "We'll go down now. Don't forget—first we'll talk about all the things we plan to do with all that money, just to throw him off guard, and then you can suddenly get the idea that you remember jerking your handkerchief out of your pocket in the game room.

"After we give him the pictures and films, he should be in a good mood. I hope we can talk him

"Tyvand and His Wife Were Arguing About Something."

into letting us go," she said. She pulled the covers
snugly over Cookie and Alexander, and then moved
two chairs next to the cots so the youngsters couldn't
roll out onto the floor.

Dagwood inspected Daisy's family, turned off all
but one small lamp, and left the door ajar as he and
Blondie braced themselves for the interview downstairs.

Dagwood did most of the talking, while Blondie
smiled encouragement and approval. Tyvand listened, uncertainty written on his face, while Mrs. Tyvand seemed plainly suspicious.

While they were talking, Tompkins, the butler,
entered the room.

"Mr. Tyvand, may I speak to you a moment, sir?"
he asked.

Dagwood sneezed, and momentarily startled, the
butler looked directly at him. Dagwood caught
Blondie's eye, and nodded to let her know that he
had confirmed his recognition of the butler.

Slightly annoyed at the interruption, Tyvand
arose, and went across the room to talk to the servant. They spoke in undertones, then the butler
came closer to Tyvand. Dagwood tried to see what
they were doing, but Tyvand blocked his view.

With a smug expression on his face, Tyvand returned to his place next to Mrs. Tyvand on the sofa.

"What were you saying?" he prompted Dagwood.

Confident that he was making progress, Dagwood exploded what he hoped was a bombshell.

"I remember now. I took my handkerchief out of my pocket when we were in the game room. If you'll wait a minute, I think I can run down there, and find the films and prints in a couple of minutes."

Blondie gave a squeal of joy.

"How nice that you thought of it, Dagwood," she said, brightly. "I am sure we'll all be glad to excuse you."

Tyvand said nothing, but puffed steadily at his cigar.

Dagwood continued, "As a matter of fact, it all comes back to me now. I can remember almost the exact spot."

Horace Tyvand began rubbing his hands together again. His wife had suddenly dropped her air of suspicion, and instead sat back, smirking.

"Prrr, prrr." Blondie said, trying to stop Dagwood from saying any more. He gave her a puzzled glance. Tyvand was about to speak.

"It strikes me as rather odd, Bumstead, that you should suddenly remember dropping the films and pictures into thin air." He stood up. "We'll decide what to do in the morning. But for now we'll say good-night!"

Bewildered, Dagwood and Blondie rose and headed for the door. Before they made their exit, it was

Tyvand who dropped the bombshell.

"It also strikes me as rather odd, Bumstead, that the missing negatives and films should be found in the mouth of the moose!"

CHAPTER ELEVEN

CAUGHT IN THE TRAP

Dolefully, Dagwood and Blondie sat on the bed in their room and tried to figure out what their next step would be.

Blondie commented, "That slimy butler must have come in with the information that the search had been successful."

"Yeah," Dagwood agreed. "Then Tyvand began playing cat and mouse again. How did you know, Blondie? You purred at me."

"I knew he had won some kind of advantage, because otherwise he would have barked at the butler for disturbing him. That was all acting, too. Those Tyvands are thick as thieves with those servants."

"Thieves is right," Dagwood said, ruefully. "And it looks as if we aren't going to be able to stop them Tyvand won't let us go until after the inquest. You can bet on that."

Blondie yawned, and wearily dropped her head on Dagwood's shoulder.

"I'm too tired to think any more now," she sighed. "But something will come to my mind before morning. And you'll think of something, too, Dagwood."

"The Bumsteads never say die!" Dagwood said.

He had meant the remark humorously, but instead of laughing, Blondie shuddered.

"At least we're all together," Blondie said, drowsily.

Dagwood yawned. "I'm dead tired, too. And I wish I had a sandwich."

That caused Blondie to smile. "For once, I'm spared that," she said, and her husband awarded her with an affectionate pat.

"I know one thing," he said, moving toward the door. "I'm going to make certain that no one gets in this room." He tried to open the door. Blondie watched him.

"It's locked, isn't it? Our host and hostess made certain that no one will get out of this room, didn't they?" she asked, and Dagwood nodded. But as a special precaution, he tugged and pushed the desk until he had it in position to block the door.

Meanwhile, Blondie searched in a closet and found two old-fashioned women's nightgowns.

"I'm not going to wear one of those!" Dagwood fretted.

"Oh, yes, you are, because that's all our host has provided," Blondie informed him. She went into the bathroom adjoining the room, and called out, "And it looks as though you're going to be forced to fake a shave with talcum powder in the morning."

Dagwood's answer was a loud snore. The moment

his head had touched the pillow, he had fallen sound asleep.

Blondie would have sworn, before she climbed into bed, that she would not get a wink of sleep, under the strange circumstances in which the Bumsteads were involved in the Brentwood Manor mystery. But being completely worn out by the nerve-wracking happenings of that eventful day, she slept soundly until the noise of her family greeting the dawn of the next morning awakened her.

She sat up with a start, and tried to shake the slumbering Dagwood.

"Phnnff!" he responded, sleepily.

"Dagwood! Wake up! I've just had an idea!"

"Phnnff!" he snorted, then rubbed his eyes. He reached out, trying to shut off the familiar alarm clock, and the surprise of finding nothing there woke him.

He sat up, startled. "Where are we?"

Blondie didn't answer, knowing that as soon as he was fully awake, he would remember his strange whereabouts. He yawned, stretched, then blinked at Blondie.

"What did you say before? Did I dream it, or did you say you had an idea?"

"I have an idea, Dagwood. It came to me when I woke up and saw the children and the dogs running around."

"Well?" Dagwood didn't seem to think that was anything to get excited about.

"The dogs and the children! They're the answer. Remember how annoyed Tyvand became when they were noisy yesterday? When we go down to breakfast, we'll just turn them loose on the house. In no time at all, the Tyvands will be only too glad to get rid of us."

"Sounds as if it might work," Dagwood said. "It won't hurt to give it a try. But what if they don't invite us down to breakfast, but bring it up to us, instead?"

"Oh, they'll let us come downstairs, I'm sure, Dagwood. We'll insist on it. We'll pound on the floor, and I'm sure Alexander and Cookie will be glad to help us," she said, slyly.

But it wasn't necessary to resort to pounding tactics, for as the Bumsteads washed and dressed, there was a tap on the door!

"What is it?" Blondie called.

"Breakfast will be served in fifteen minutes," the voice of Tompkins reported.

"We'll be there," Dagwood shouted, with a victorious ring in his voice.

He coached Alexander on how he wanted him to act.

"Run around with the dogs, and try to make them all yelp at once. That will make Cookie holler."

They Told Alexander What He Was to Do

"But why, Daddy? Don't we want these people to like us?" Alexander asked.

"No. We want them to not like us so much that they'll ask us to go home."

"But then they won't invite us to come again," Alexander replied, puzzled at his father's attitude.

"So much the better, Alexander. Now don't ask any more questions. Do as I say, and after we get home, I'll give you a quarter."

Alexander pouted. "I'd rather have the polo ponies, but a quarter is better than nothing," he grumbled.

"Good boy," his father applauded. "Are we all ready? Wait until you've had your breakfast before you start shouting."

With those orders ringing in their ears, the Bumstead division marched out of the room and descended the stairs.

Much to Blondie's surprise, she found that a lavish breakfast had been prepared. The Tyvands did not appear at all during the meal. Dagwood cast apprehensive glances toward the hallway, and had a glimpse of his host passing rapidly through the corridor.

"At least he's in the building," he told Blondie. "In a few minutes, we can start giving him the works."

The puppies and Daisy had been herded into the

kitchen to be fed. Then the maid opened the back door, and they all ran out.

"That spoils the plan," Dagwood said.

"They'll be back. Alexander can call them," Blondie decided.

But the Bumsteads had another disappointment coming to them.

The puppies came in when they were called, and the children ran around the house, squealing and yelling. The Tyvands stood it as long as they could. Blondie and Dagwood hopefully awaited orders to get out with their noisy tribe.

Instead, it wasn't long before the Bumsteads, children, dogs and all, found themselves back in their sleeping room.

"You can't do this to us," Dagwood told Tyvand. "We know our rights."

Exasperated, their host mopped his brow.

"Rights or no rights, you keep that wild Indian tribe in here until they calm down."

Blondie said, "But they want to go home."

"They can go home, and you can go home this afternoon. You don't think I'm going to be fool enough to let you go while there's still a chance that Dagwood Bumstead will show up at the inquest, do you?"

"But you said—" Blondie began.

"Never mind what I said," was the curt rejoinder.

"Your husband was wily enough to hide the films and prints, wasn't he?"

Dagwood beamed. "That was pretty clever of me, wasn't it?"

But Tyvand was not in an appreciative mood. He glowered at Dagwood.

Blondie decided to use different tactics.

"Supposing Mr. Bumstead decides to see the coroner tomorrow," Blondie said, coyly.

A cutting laugh preceded Tyvand's reply. "It has occurred to me to mention at the inquest that I have photographs of the crash. There are two of the four which are quite harmless. As a matter of fact, they may be quite a help to us, because it shows my witnesses among the group of people around the wrecked car."

"The license number on your car shows," Dagwood said, "if you will recall."

Tyvand laughed shortly. "Do you think I would be stupid enough to produce that one?"

Crestfallen, Dagwood and Blondie gave up trying to convince Tyvand that they should be permitted to leave his luxurious home.

Tyvand seemed to be enjoying himself. "What s more, when I tell the jury that the man who took the pictures wanted me to pay a thousand dollars for them, they won't have much sympathy for him."

"But I didn't ask you for a thousand dollars! You

offered it to me!" Dagwood exclaimed.

"Will they believe that? Especially when the insurance companies tell them that you ignored the offers they made you?"

"How did you know about the insurance companies offering me any money for the snapshots?" Dagwood asked. "I'm sure I didn't tell you about them."

"There are many ways of obtaining information," Tyvand replied cryptically.

Blondie stopped Dagwood from saying anything more. She turned on Tyvand.

"I think you are the most thoroughly detestable man I ever met," she said, simply.

Tyvand responded with an elaborate bow.

"And I am sure you are the most charming prisoner Brentwood Manor has ever confined," he sneered.

Blondie turned her back on him and stalked over to the front window. Dagwood spluttered, trying to find words cutting enough to address to his host, but before he could utter them, Tyvand had left the room. He closed the door, and they heard the noise of the key turning in the lock.

A short time later, there was a tap at the door. Tompkins, the butler, entered, pushing a tea cart heaped with dishes.

"Your luncheon," he informed them.

"It isn't time to eat yet, is it?" Blondie said, astonished.

He didn't answer, but shut the door again, and locked it.

Dagwood said, "I'd like to push that guy down the steps."

"Why did he bring the lunch now, I wonder?" Blondie asked.

"They'll probably be too busy getting ready for their masquerade to bother about it later."

That offered a small ray of hope, Blondie thought. "At least it tells us one thing—there will be no one in the manor but the Bumsteads, after they all leave to go to the inquest."

Dagwood shook his head regretfully. "And the most important witness of all will be cooped up in here."

"And the most important evidence is where we can't get at it," Blondie added.

They agreed that the situation looked hopeless, at least at that moment.

Then Blondie perked up.

"Wait until they leave, Dagwood. Then we'll try to think of something."

"Not me," Dagwood said, ruefully. "My mind's a blank."

Alexander paused in his work of wrestling with Daisy.

"What's a blank?" he asked.

Blondie answered. "That's what your Daddy drew when he tried to cash in with his camera," she informed her son.

CHAPTER TWELVE

THE RESCUE

Blondie and Dagwood watched the Tyvand automobile as it appeared from the rear of the estate, and stopped in front of the big iron gate.

"They're all in there," Blondie commented. "Tompkins, in his witness clothes, is getting out to open the gate. Horace the Horrible is sitting in the front seat. Henrietta, the horse-face, is sitting in the back with Maggie, the monster, and the blitzkrieg woman in the green coat."

"Don't try to be funny," Dagwood groaned. "Let's hope he forgets to lock the gate."

Tompkins didn't forget to lock the gate. He waited while Tyvand took the driver's seat and drove the car through the archway, and the heavy gate swung shut with a loud, doleful clang. Then he resumed his place at the wheel, and Tyvand was again at his side.

"That's that!" Blondie said.

But the sound of the gate clanging shut aroused and angered Dagwood. His drooping spirits revived.

"That is not that!" he said. "I belong in that witness chair, and that's where I'm going to be this afternoon!"

Alexander began to clap, and Cookie pat-a-caked with him. "That's a nice speech, Daddy," Alexander cried.

"But we can't talk our way out of here," Blondie wailed.

"No, but we can *act*," Dagwood said.

He looked at the big front window in such a determined manner that Blondie thought for a minute he was going to make a running jump through it.

"Stop!" Blondie squealed.

"What?" Dagwood dazedly replied.

"Don't jump through the window," Blondie cautioned.

Disgustedly, Dagwood informed her that he had no intention of jumping through the window. He was examining it to see if it could be opened.

"What good will that do? We can't climb down a flat wall."

"That's right," Dagwood admitted. "And if we did climb down the manor wall, there's no way to get over the stone fence."

"Are you positive about that, Dagwood? What did you find out last night when you hunted for the puppies?"

Dagwood sat down, trying to recall exactly what had happened.

"Oh, I remember now," he exclaimed. "I came to

another gate. It was locked, too. And Elmer was on the other side of it."

"But how did he get inside again?"

"He scrooched down and crawled under it."

Quickly, Blondie ran to the front window again and looked at the front gate.

"I'll bet he could get under the front gate, too. Now if we could only think of a way to get him down there . . ." she paused.

"But, Blondie, he'd only run around the street for awhile, and then he'd run home, if he decided he didn't want to come back here. Then we'd have him to worry about on top of everything else."

"Quiet, Dagwood. Let's not talk so much and think harder."

Alexander had been listening intently. "Can I think, too, Mama?"

"Yes, dear," Blondie said, absently.

Dagwood was sitting in a chair, his chin in hand. His son promptly sat in a chair and assumed the same pose.

"I thought the hardest," Alexander announced. "I just thought of what to do with Elmer. Hang a sign on him, telling people to make him come back here."

"That's it, Blondie! Hang a sign on him!"

"How silly," Blondie responded. "If all we wanted to do was to get him back here, we might as well

Alexander Assumed Dagwood's Pose

keep him here in the first place!"

Dagwood was excited, and began waving his arms and walking up and down, thinking aloud as he planned.

"The sign can say 'HELP' in big red letters," he announced.

Alexander laughed. "We haven't any red crayons," he told his father, importantly.

"Lipstick! We can write it in lipstick!" Blondie exclaimed.

"Then we'll write a note, and tie it around his neck," Dagwood continued. Then he halted. "But who should we write it to? The police will think I've gone crazy, just as they've always suspected."

Blondie began pacing the floor. "Oh, dear, if we could only think of someone to get in touch with!"

"Someone who could easily be located by whoever opened the note," Dagwood added.

Alexander produced another idea. "Put it in the newspaper," he said.

Blondie hugged him. "Alexander, you're too bright for one boy. You should be twins! We can't put it in the newspaper, but it gives me an idea!"

"Pete Howard, the reporter!" Dagwood shouted at the top of his voice.

"You try to get the window open, while I try to write out the note," Blondie instructed. "We've got to work fast."

"Can I tear up a sheet for a rope, like they do in the movies?" Alexander begged.

"Yes, dear," Blondie said. "But Daddy will have to help you, because we're in a big hurry."

Alexander jumped up and down gleefully.

"We're captives, just like Cowboy Joe from Kokomo! Only he sent for the G-men and they caught a den of dope-smugglers. Who are we trying to catch?"

"A gang of crooks," Dagwood said.

"Goody!" Alexander said, delightedly.

"It won't be 'goody' if we don't get out of here, young man. And we've got to depend on little Elmer to turn the trick," his mother informed him.

Blondie finished writing the urgent note, telling whoever found Elmer to get in touch immediately with Pete Howard, police reporter of the *News*. They were to ask him to go to Brentwood Manor, Shorecrest, where Dagwood Bumstead, X-34, was in peril. She read the note aloud.

"Are you in peril, Daddy?" Alexander said, hopefully.

"Not exactly, but this is a pretty serious case, my boy. We want him to hurry. Have you the big sign ready, Blondie?"

Blondie held up the placard, made from the top of the stationery box, and it bore the one word HELP in big red lettering.

They had to call on Alexander to help hold the squirming Elmer while they fastened the notes and the sign around his fat body by means of a harness fashioned from two curtain cords.

They tested the strength of the sheet-rope by pulling on it.

"Elmer, everything depends on you," Blondie whispered to the puppy, as she tied the sheet lengths to the harness.

Elmer felt far from noble. He twisted and tugged, trying to free himself. Even Daisy seemed concerned, and barked inquisitively. Alexander assured the big dog that everything was going to be okay.

They cautiously, but hurriedly, carried out their plan. Both Dagwood and Blondie held the rope, while they gently lowered Elmer, loudly protesting, down the front of the building.

Dagwood groaned. "Gosh! We forgot about the sheet! How are we going to get it unfastened?"

"We can't!" Blondie gasped. "He'll just have to take it along with him."

"Will that look funny—like a kite tail," Alexander said.

"Don't worry about that part of it," Blondie reassured the other two. "The funnier he looks, the better, because then he will attract attention."

They boosted Alexander and Cookie up to the window, where they could get a view of Elmer.

With baited breath, the Bumsteads, framed in the big window, watched every move that Elmer made. They frantically began calling out the window to him, because he joyfully pranced around the lawn, then headed for the back yard.

Dagwood held Daisy up to the window, and instructed her to bark at her unruly offspring. Daisy didn't want to bark, but Alexander solved the problem by making her speak for a bit of leftover meat.

Elmer appeared in view again. The sign was still intact, and the long white streamer trailed along behind him.

"Go home!" Blondie shouted. He sat there, provocatively looking up at them.

"Go home!" Dagwood yelled, and there was a genuine note of appeal in his voice.

Elmer, after tugging in vain at the trailing strips of sheeting, started down the roadway leading to the front gate. Again the Bumsteads waited breathlessly.

"If I had him here, I'd thrash him!'" Dagwood muttered through gnashing teeth.

"I'd hug him, Dagwood. Look! He's crawling under the gate, now!" Blondie exclaimed.

But that was as far as he got. It was hard to distinguish exactly what happened from their distant vantage point, but apparently the loose end of the sheet trailer had become tangled in the bars at the bottom of the gate. Elmer was on the other side of the gate, but that was all. He could move only a short distance.

The Bumsteads could shout as loud and as long as they wanted to, but no amount of calling could free Elmer from the tangle.

Dagwood closed the window, and he and Blondie dejectedly came back into the center of the room and slumped into the nearest chairs.

Blondie picked up Cookie and hummed to her, and the baby soon fell asleep.

Tragically, Dagwood stared into space. Alexander, boylike, was only momentarily taken aback, and then recouped by playing a game with Daisy and the four girl-puppies.

Time dragged. Ten minutes seemed like ten hours.

"Soon it will be too late to do anything," Dagwood moaned.

"Not only that, but if your name is brought up at the inquest, Tyvand will twist the evidence around to make you look bad," Blondie said.

Suddenly Alexander, who had been watching at the window, called them to come over there.

"Elmer's gone!" he said.

Dagwood opened the window again.

They listened, and soon, to their disappointment, heard an excited yapping. They looked beneath the

Alexander Played a Noisy Game With the Puppies

window, and there stood Elmer.

"The sign is gone," Blondie pointed out.

"So is the fancy harness," Dagwood said. "He probably tugged until he extricated himself from it at the gate."

They peered toward the driveway entrance.

"I think I see it," Blondie exclaimed.

"Is it inside or outside?"

"Outside. How do you suppose it got there? Do you think he dragged it, or do you think . . ." Blondie was afraid to express her hope aloud.

Dagwood held up one hand, fingers crossed. "Here's hoping." he said. "We'll soon find out."

The distant ringing of the telephone could be heard.

"Maybe that's Pete Howard calling now!" Blondie fervently wished aloud.

Whoever was calling let the telephone ring for a long time, as if to make certain that there was no one at home.

"We'll watch out the window, now. Let's hang a bright blanket, or something, out of the window, to attract his attention if he does come!"

They found a patchwork quilt. The underside of it was bright red.

"This should do it," Blondie decided.

Trembling with excitement, she helped Dagwood hold it out of the window. Again, the minutes dragged.

Alexander was the first to notice a car speeding down the street leading to Brentwood Manor. Dagwood and Blondie frantically waved the quilt, almost tearing it apart in their excitement. The car stopped in front of the big iron gate, and a man jumped out. He tried to open the big door and the smaller built-in door. He shook them with all his might.

"Now we're getting somewhere," Blondie sighed, happily.

They strained their eyes to watch the man's movements. He went to the rear of his car, opened the trunk, and pulled out a long towrope.

Looping it over one of the pickets on the top of the stone fence, the man climbed to the top. He scrambled over the pickets, hauled up the rope, and dropped it on the inner side of the wall.

Using the rope to lower himself, the man was soon on the ground, and running in the direction of the house. Abruptly he turned, and went back for the rope.

Dagwood heaved a sigh of relief. "I was afraid he was going to forget that," he remarked.

"I'm so thrilled!" Blondie said. "I think we're still in time to get to the inquest."

"And will we throw a bomb in Horace the Horrible's face!" Dagwood grinned. "While he's run-

ning up here, I'll tie a couple of sheets together, so
we can haul up his rope."

Blondie waited at the window.

"Are you Pete Howard?" she called down.

"That's me!" was the answer from below. "How
many of you are there up there?"

"Nine of us!" Blondie yelled.

"Nine people?" was the astonished interrogation.

"No. Two adults, two children, and five dogs."

Dagwood leaned out of the window with the tied
sheets, and he and the reporter conferred on how to
get them all out of the house.

"I could smash in a window down here, if you're
being held illegally," Pete called.

"That wouldn't help," Dagwood informed him.
"The door is locked up here, and the key is gone."

So they decided that the Bumsteads would all
have to be lowered out of the window.

"Throw the quilt down, and we can use it to catch
the boy after everyone is down. Is he scared?"

"Who, me?" Alexander scoffed. "I can stay here,
and then untie the rope. Then you can catch me
like firemen catching somebody in a net."

Pete Howard's low laugh floated up. "Bright boy
you got there, Bumstead."

"Thanks! But we've got to hurry. We have to get
to that Billingate inquest before it's all over," Dagwood shouted.

"It's almost over now! I just came from there. But maybe we can make it. Send your wife and the little girl down first, then you come down. The three of us can hold the blanket, and the boy will have to toss the dogs, one by one, into the quilt. Then the boy can jump. Can he do that?" the reporter called up to them.

"Can I do it? You just watch me!" Alexander yelled, with enthusiasm.

Meanwhile, Dagwood had fastened a harness-swing device with the sheet around Blondie, tied the rope to it, and as she sat on the windowsill, he gently placed the sleeping Cookie in her arms.

With Pete Howard calling instructions from below, and Dagwood from above, Blondie and Cookie finally reached the ground. Dagwood followed, carrying Daisy in one arm. He wound the rope around one leg, and then gripped it with his free hand, loosening his grip to descend slowly.

"When I was a boy, I shinnied up and down ropes like a monkey," Dagwood boasted.

There was considerable scrambling before Alexander finally got all the pups tossed into the blanket held by Dagwood and Pete Howard.

When it came Alexander's turn, after he had unfastened the rope, he had a moment of stage fright before he leaped.

The three waiting below shouted encouragement.

"Come on, Cowboy Joe from Kokomo!" Blondie said. That was the right note to strike, and Alexander jumped.

"How are we going to get over the wall?" Blondie was anxious to know.

"Let's hurry down there," Dagwood urged. "We'll figure that out when we get there."

Pete Howard worked out the solution. Using the towrope, he got on top of the wall. Dagwood fastened the rope around Blondie and boosted her up. She was still holding Cookie, and there was a perilous moment, as Pete lowered her on the other side, when it was almost too much for his strength. With a jolt, Blondie landed on the ground, but she was smiling in relief, and trying to quiet Cookie, who was voicing loud objections to the whole business. Next came Alexander and Daisy; after that Dagwood shooed the pups under the gate before he climbed the rope. He and Pete Howard quickly descended, and helped herd the Bumstead group into Pete's car.

"Where to?" Pete Howard wanted to know. "Someone give some directions, and then you can explain a few things to me while we go wherever we're going."

"Head for the courthouse first," Dagwood told the reporter.

"But you haven't got the snapshot that will clinch

He Shooed the Pups Under the Gate

our evidence, Dagwood," Blondie said.

"If I'm at the inquest, I can stall them while you and Pete go after it," Dagwood answered. "I've got to go up there and filibuster until you can find the picture and get to the courthouse."

Blondie had a few questions she wanted to ask the reporter.

"Tell us how you happened to find us. Did you find Elmer?"

"Who's Elmer?"

"Elmer is the boy puppy. We had the note to you tied onto him," Dagwood explained.

"Well, luckily, the newsboy who peddles this area found the note. He knew me, called the office, and had them get in touch with me immediately," Pete explained.

"It was nice of you to come right away," Blondie said, with a grateful smile.

"You two are pretty clever, do you know it?" Pete grinned. "When I stopped in at the police station this morning, the boys were talking about some screwball, or bunch of screwballs, who kept calling up and asking if the police station was the Dagwood Bumstead residence. Then they said that my name had been mentioned. I pinned them down on exactly what was said, and when the sarge said, in falsetto tones, 'EX-cuse me, I've tried three or four times to do something or other,' that 'X-34" clicked

with me, because I had a hunch there was a story behind that blind ad you put in the paper, and had
written another answer to it today. Now you tell me
your story."

"Blondie can tell you all about it when she gets
the picture of Cookie that we have at home," Dagwood said. "We're almost to the courthouse now.
Just let me out."

"Can I go, too, Daddy?" Alexander pleaded. "I
want to hear you make a speech."

"They're going to try to make your Daddy look
awfully silly, son," Dagwood said. "Are you sure
you want to see that?"

"I want to clap when you make your speech," the
boy responded.

Blondie knew Dagwood would rather go alone,
so she promised Alexander that he could go up to
the courtroom later, when she and the reporter
finished their errand.

"Good luck, dear," Blondie whispered, and Dagwood left the car and dashed up the courthouse
steps.

Pete Howard was burning up with curiosity, and
questioned Blondie closely about the Bumsteads
and their connection with the Billingate affair.

He whistled in amazement, when she presented
all the clues she and Dagwood had rounded up during their forced visit at the manor, and linked them

to the ones they already had through the series of queer happenings at their home preceding the time they left to meet the mysterious writer of the letter to Dagwood.

"How did you happen to withhold the one picture that would do those schemers the most harm?" he wanted to know.

"We didn't do that on purpose. Dagwood meant to play square with the person he sold the pictures to. And Tyvand made his offer big enough, or hinted that he was going to pay a large enough amount, that he could be quite certain that Dagwood wouldn't hold out on him. I was the one that kept the film of Cookie, and the one of the puppies at the picnic, from the ones Dagwood developed that night."

"Do you think Horace Tyvand has any inkling that you have it to spring on him?"

"Oh, no. Besides, he thinks we're safely locked in the manor," Blondie assured him.

"Do you think he sent someone to your house to look for the films?"

"He must have—several times. I think that tramp, or Tompkins, as he turned out to be later, and the cleaning woman both hunted for them."

Pete Howard shook his head. He couldn't understand how Blondie could find a hiding place that a pseudo-cleaning woman couldn't find.

"I merely placed the blotting book containing the prints and films under the Dutch oven," she said, simply.

He laughed heartily. "She must have been within inches of them, without knowing it."

Blondie laughed too, as she reflected how clever the woman had been about getting into the house as a cleaning woman. She had dismissed Mrs. Swenson, who had been sent by the employment bureau and pretended that she couldn't speak English. But with all her cleverness she had failed in her main objective.

"I'll bet Tyvand had a hectic time trying to figure out how to make his letter convincing and enticing enough to make Dagwood want to look into it further," Howard commented.

"It was cleverly written," Blondie admitted readily.

Pete Howard brought the car to a halt in front of the Bumstead home. Alexander and the dogs rushed pell-mell out of the car and ran around the front lawn.

"I wish we could go in there now and settle down for a quiet, uneventful evening," Blondie said, wistfully.

"I'm sorry, Mrs. Bumstead, but I can't let you follow your inclinations now. We've got your husband down there filibustering his head off, remember?"

"That's right. Mr. Howard. And I have a feeling that he s going to run out of words any minute now."

CHAPTER THIRTEEN

IN THE WITNESS CHAIR

Pete Howard was delighted with the picture Blondie gave him.

"This will convict Tyvand and his accomplices of one of the most heartless acts ever performed in this town," he exclaimed. "The first thing we must do is go down to my office, while I have enlargements made of the film. I'll have one made for the coroner's jury, and another for the evening edition of the *News*."

"But we won't have time for that," Blondie protested. "Dagwood is talking on and on, trying to stall until we get there!"

"Can't be helped," was the reply. "I've a hunch that this Tyvand is pretty clever, and by this time he will have your husband so tangled up in his own words, he'll begin to think that *he* perpetrated the crime."

"In that case, shouldn't we rush there," Blondie pleaded, "and not bother right now about the enlargements?"

"Calm down, Mrs. Bumstead," the reporter said soothingly. "If I know my public officials, it will be much to your husband's advantage if we have every bit of our information gathered before we try to present it."

"I do hope you're right," Blondie said, worriedly. She was about to replace the other snapshots, when Pete asked if he might have them, too.

"If you wish," Blondie said. "We certainly are under obligation to you for helping us through this mess."

"Forget about that angle," Pete Howard suggested. "I'm getting a whale of a yarn out of it, and it'll be a feather in my cap."

Blondie gathered Cookie and Alexander near her, preparing to leave the house and re-enter Pete's automobile.

"Daisy can stay here and look after her pups until we get back," she said.

But Pete would have none of that.

"I want all of you to be in the courtroom when this drama reaches its grand finale," he insisted. "I don't want anyone left out of it."

So again, not only the children but the dogs were included in Dagwood's and Blondie's strange adventure. Blondie explained that she and her husband had often found themselves in odd situations, but this would be the first time all ten members of the family group would not only attend but participate in an inquest called by a coroner. It was an unusual situation, even for the Bumsteads.

Blondie, Cookie, Alexander, and the dogs waited as patiently as possible outside the newspaper office, while Pete Howard went into the *News* building with the pictures.

Blondie uneasily noticed the time in a near-by store window, and had visions of Dagwood, hoarse-voiced and perspiring, trying to hold the Tyvands, their attorneys, the coroner, and the jury at bay while waiting desperately for his wife to come to his rescue.

She patted Cookie, who was restless, and said aloud, "You aren't any more tired of all this than I am, baby girl. I have a good notion to take your Daddy's camera out in the back yard and bury it. after this is all over."

Cookie gazed at her mother with wide, childish wonder, in so serious a manner that Blondie could scarcely keep from laughing.

Pete Howard's voice said, "You're a good waiter, Mrs. Bumstead." He had observed her amused expression, and informed her that ninety-nine out of a hundred women under the same circumstances would be shrieking and tearing their hair in frantic impatience.

Blondie laughed appreciatively. "I'm not shrieking and tearing my hair, but I can well imagine that Dagwood is almost to that stage. For all we know, they might have had him arrested and clapped in jail by this time."

"If he is, we'll get him out of there, don't worry. There's just one thing I want to ask of you as a favor. Promise me that you won't say or do anything at the courthouse until I give you the signal. Promise?"

"You seem to be running the show pretty well," Blondie smiled. "I won't do anything until I hear from you."

Blondie was a woman of her word. She had made the promise, and felt honor-bound to keep it, although within the next half hour there were a few uneasy moments when she regretted having made the promise.

Pete Howard apparently had some influence in the courthouse. He pulled a few official strings and soon he and Blondie, Alexander and Cookie, Daisy and her five puppies all filed past the guard into the courtroom.

Instead of finding Dagwood shrieking and tearing his hair, they found him talking calmly. The coroner apparently was gnashing his teeth in fury as he glared at the man in the witness chair.

"In all my public career, Bumstead, I have never encountered a man who could sit in a witness chair, vow to tell the truth, and then tell such abominable lies with such supreme self-confidence," the official barked.

They All Filed into the Courtroom

"But I'm telling the truth. The truth never hurt anyone like it's going to hurt Horace the Horrible and Henrietta the Horseface, as my wife laughingly describes them. That reminds me of the time when Blondie . . ."

Dagwood was interrupted by the increasingly irate coroner again.

"Never mind any more stories of your intimate home life!" he shouted. "The more you talk, the more evident it is to the men and women of the jury that you are mentally deranged. We have already had three eye-witnesses testify. Their testimony coincides, and none of it faintly resembles the wild tale of farcial comedy that you are trying to pawn off on us. What's more, it has been pointed out, with substantial proof, that whatever connection you had in this affair was from a purely monetary angle. You trample on the grief of the bereaved, thinking only of your own financial betterment . . ."

Dagwood snorted in contempt, looking Tyvand straight in the eye. Tyvand dropped his eyes to some papers in front of him.

"You're going to be sorry if you don't take my word for it," Dagwood said. "You'll find out that I'm telling the truth."

Alexander, in the back of the room, whispered to his mother, "Isn't Daddy wonderful?" Blondie agreed.

When the coroner warned Dagwood that there were libel laws and perjury laws and defamation of character laws, Blondie began to fidget. She looked hopefully at Pete Howard, who sat back, relaxed and at ease, obviously enjoying the whole procedure immensely.

"Can't we help him now?" Blondie begged. "This sounds like real trouble."

Pete shook his head and whispered, "That guy is getting too puffed up—the coroner, I mean. I want to wait until the psychological moment before I stick a pin in him."

That caught Alexander's attention. "Can I stick a pin in him, too?" he demanded.

Pete snickered, and Blondie hastily whispered that Mr. Howard didn't mean a *real* pin, but an imaginary one.

"Will he say 'ouch'?" Alexander asked.

Pete chuckled again. "That he will," he informed the boy.

The coroner seemed bent on putting Dagwood in as bad a light as possible. He orated on the subject of cranks, and how one is sure to pop up on every important occasion. He dramatically pointed a finger at Dagwood.

"Why this—this self-appointed buttinsky—this conceited, penny-pinching opportunist—this egotistical wind-bag—" Words failed him. He paused, and said, sarcastically, "And he expects to appear here and besmirch the integrity of these good people—" his sweeping gesture took in the Tyvands, who modestly lowered their heads, "without a shred of evidence to back up or support his fantastic story!" His voice had reached a high crescendo. Dagwood was looking at Blondie, and they were smiling at each other understandingly. The coroner seemed a bit nonplussed at Dagwood's seeming indifference to his tirade.

In an undertone, Pete Howard said, "This is as good a time as any." He handed her a folder. "The picture is inside. Present it to the loudspeaker. That should tone him down somewhat!"

Blondie peeked into the folder for a glimpse of the photo enlargement. Then she rose, still carrying Cookie in her arms, and headed toward the witness stand.

Alexander promptly got up from his seat, too. Not to be outdone, Daisy and the puppies, who had been unobtrusively lying under the bench seats, got to their feet, too. Pete Howard signaled to the *News* cameraman.

There was a ripple of laughter, an exclamation, and a gasp from the assemblage as Blondie led her family through the courtroom. All the Bumsteads, human and canine, were ready for the climax.

"Now what?" the coroner exclaimed in exasperation. "Don't tell me this—this menagerie belongs to *you!*"

He glowered at Dagwood.

"Hello, Blondie," Dagwood said, ignoring the man. "Did you bring it?"

Blondie nodded.

Horace Tyvand jumped to his feet.

"My wife and I have had about all of this that we can stand!" he snapped. "We would like to ask a postponement, or an adjournment, or—or anything to get out of here. It has been an extremely trying day for us."

Dagwood laughed. "Not nearly as trying as it's going to be, my false friend." He held out his hand, and Blondie placed the picture folder in it.

Without further word, Dagwood extracted the picture, and studied it. "Not bad," he commented, satisfaction in his tone. "My little old black box of an almost-human camera turned out to be a friend in need."

"And a friend indeed," Blondie added, with a giggle.

The whole situation was changed. The coroner heard Dagwood's story again. This time he listened respectfully. The Tyvands looked about the courtroom uneasily. They knew that their little game was over.

The snapshot was conclusive proof of Horace

Tyvand's implication in the death, of his aunt. Sure-
ly he had greatly underestimated the ingenuity of
the combined Bumstead family. He and his accomplices must now bear the full brunt of the law.

CHAPTER FOURTEEN

THE CAMERA EXPERT

The pompous coroner, the suave attorneys, and the scheming Tyvand coterie of plotters were all properly deflated, much to the satisfaction and amusement of Pete Howard. At first inclined to be skeptical, the coroner suspected that Dagwood might have faked the picture. But Pete Howard's announcement that the entire story, plus pictures of the Bumstead family and the tell-tale view of the accident, would appear splashed all over the *News* evening edition, convinced the official that the picture was genuine.

Satisfied that their part of the performance was at an end, the Bumsteads withdrew from the court-room, but not before a general search for Elmer, who had curled up in a corner for a snooze.

Pete Howard escorted them to his car and drove them to their home.

"You'll be famous," Pete promised. "They'll be wanting to award you a merit badge and a key to the city."

"But I don't want a merit badge and a key to the city," Dagwood informed him.

"Why not? What do you want, the nine dollars I

owe you for your snapshots?" he asked jokingly.

"Nope," Dagwood said. "The less I see and hear about the pictures the better I will like it. All I want is some information from Blondie."

"What do you want to know?" his wife asked.

"All I want to know is this—what are we going to have for supper?"

The Bumstead homestead was not long in hitting its normal stride.

Blondie pleased and appeased her hungry husband with a pork chop dinner and banana cream pie for dessert. But even this did not stop him from getting his usual evening sandwich idea.

He snapped his fingers. "I've got a great idea for a sandwich—a slice of onion between every layer," he announced.

Blondie found him in the kitchen.

"You're crying, dear! What's the matter?" she inquired sympathetically.

"Nothing. I'm just peeling an onion," Dagwood answered tearfully.

That gave Blondie an idea, and she ran out of the kitchen with the remark, "It's a shame to waste all those tears."

She reappeared a moment later, and handed the tearful Dagwood a slip of paper. "As long as you're crying, here's the bill for my new coat," she said

Dagwood Scowled at the Bill

with a twinkle in her eye. .

Dagwood scowled at the bill, but soon forgot it
as he tried out his new sandwich, pointing out that
it was good to be home again in their cozy little
place.

"You couldn't pay me to be a millionaire," he
boasted.

He wandered around the house casting appreciative glances at his possessions. He went down to the
basement, thankful that now he had nothing to tear
down there.

Later, he tested the temperature of the hot-water
tank with his palm.

"Ah-h. Just enough hot water for a nice, sizzling
bath," he gloated.

He dashed upstairs to fill the bathtub.

"It's just right—Now, I'll take off my clothes while
the tub fills up."

He went to his room and undressed in less than
five minutes. But that was too long, for upon his return, he found the bathroom occupied. Blondie was
calmly taking a bath.

"*Hey!*" he shouted. "I filled up that tub for myself!"

"It's all in the family, dear. It's not as though you
were finding a total stranger in the tub," she soothed.

Grudgingly, Dagwood put on his clothes again.

This time he used a different inflection in his voice when he remarked, "There's no place like home."

He changed his mind about dressing, and decided to crawl into his own comfortable bed. When Blondie finished her bath, she came in and found his trousers hung on a chair, one leg dragging on the floor, and the other dangling over the top of the chair.

"Dagwood Bumstead! Just look at your trousers, she scolded. "You should hang them on a hanger when you go to bed."

She proceeded to hang them up herself. "I hung them on the chair," Dagwood defended himself sleepily.

"You didn't hang them on the chair! You threw them at the chair!" she argued.

Dagwood sat up in bed, highly indignant. "Gee whiz—you talk as though I threw them on the floor!" he complained.

Blondie dropped the argument, and wearily climbed into bed only to be disturbed later by Dagwood jumping up to grab the fly swatter. He was after the one lone mosquito that buzzed around his head.

He reached up to swat the insect, which swooped down and came to rest on the wall in back of Dagwood. In his excitement, Dagwood took a wild swing, flopped over backwards, and landed on his feet.

"Well, what do you know about that?" he cried. Blondie turned to see what had made him so happy, just in time to see him flop over again, proudly informing her that he could turn back-flips.

Blondie laughed. "Pete Howard should put that in the paper, too. 'Dagwood Bumstead discovers he can turn back-flips while swatting a mosquito.'"

Sheepishly, Dagwood crawled under the covers and was soon contentedly snoring.

The strange adventure of the Bumsteads and how they extricated themselves from it was widely publicized, and Dagwood basked in the limelight for several days.

His bid for fame had at least one satisfactory result—the knowledge that the evil schemes of the Tyvands had been thwarted, and the victim of their machinations had been avenged.

And there was a secondary satisfaction—Mr. Dithers not only forgave him for taking a day off without permission, but declined to dock him for it.

Dagwood was also guest of honor at a meeting of a camera club, which presented him with a movie camera, along with compliments on the pictures of the puppies at the picnic, which Pete Howard had published in the paper for their human interest value.

Dagwood also had the pleasure of hearing the police sergeant call himself a nitwit for not paying attention to Dagwood when he had telephoned.

Young Alexander, mentioning with regret to Alvin that he just missed owning a string of polo
ponies, comforted himself by telling his chum a long
and exciting account of his leap from the window of
the manor, which grew in height with each telling,
until it dwarfed the town's tallest skyscraper.

Cookie finished her role in the dramatic episode
by having her sleeping hours thrown off schedule.
Dagwood wore himself out trying to quiet her because he couldn't "stand to hear a woman cry."

Daisy and her five rambunctious puppies settled
back to normal living immediately. The puppies began by chewing up Dagwood's new slippers. Elmer
showed his appreciation of having his picture in the
paper by holding up a paw and punching a hole
through the sheet as they held it up to show him
how he looked.

Blondie was thankful when the hubbub died
down. She rewarded herself for her part in the adventure by purchasing a new hat.

Alexander was amazed to find her wearing it
around the house.

"Why are you wearing your new hat in the
kitchen, Mama?" he asked.

"So Papa will be sure and notice it when he comes

home," she explained.

Dagwood came into the kitchen a short time later. "Hello, dear," he said as he kissed her. He went over to the stove, lifted the cover of the stewpan, and sniffed appreciatively.

Blondie inquired, "Dagwood, don't you notice something new?"

Instead of noticing Blondie's new, chic headdress, her tactless husband, very much pleased, answered, "Yeh. You've got some mushrooms in the stew to day."

But Blondie had the laugh on him later. Still in flated by all of the praise he had received for his prowess with the camera, Dagwood decided to spend his spare minutes taking more pictures.

Blondie was too busy, and Alexander went out to play with Alvin. Cookie was asleep, and the dogs had chased after Alexander. There was no one about to pose for Dagwood.

. But Dagwood was not to be thwarted that easily. When Blondie peered in the living room to see what Dagwood was doing, she was amused to find Mr. Beasley, the mailman, sitting in a chair, while Dag wood took angle shots of him.

"I certainly appreciate this, Mr. Beasley," Dag wood was saying.

"That's all right, Bumstead," responded the post man, with an airy wave of his hand. "It's all part of the service."

This peaceful life was a far cry from the excitement of a few days before, but to all of the Bumsteads, it was a more comfortable and satisfactory existence.